PUSHIN' UP DAISIES

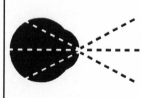

This Large Print Book carries the
Seal of Approval of N.A.V.H.

A BLACK SWAN HISTORICAL ROMANCE

Pushin' Up Daisies

Carolyn Brown

THORNDIKE PRESS

A part of Gale, Cengage Learning

Detroit • New York • San Francisco • New Haven, Conn • Waterville, Maine • London

GALE
CENGAGE Learning™

Copyright © 2009 by Carolyn Brown.
A Black Swan Historical Romance #1.
Thorndike Press, a part of Gale, Cengage Learning.

LIBRARY OF CONGRESS CATALOGING-IN-PUBLICATION DATA

Brown, Carolyn, 1948–
    Pushin' up daisies / by Carolyn Brown.
      p. cm. — (Thorndike Press large print gentle romance) (A black swan historical romance ; no. 1)
    ISBN-13: 978-1-4104-2017-6 (alk. paper)
    ISBN-10: 1-4104-2017-5 (alk. paper)
    1. Hotelkeepers—Fiction. 2. Private investigators—Fiction. 3. Missing persons—Fiction. 4. World War, 1914–1918—Fiction. 5. Arkansas—Fiction. 6. Large type books. I. Title.
    PS3552.R685275P88 2009b
    813'.54—dc22   2009028222

Published in 2009 by arrangement with Thomas Bouregy & Co., Inc.

Printed in the United States of America
1 2 3 4 5 6 7 13 12 11 10 09

To my friend Nancy J. Parra
Thank you so much!

CHAPTER ONE

The road from Strong to Huttig, Arkansas ran south and then peeled off at a forty–five degree angle a mile or so from down town. The Black Swan hotel sat on the south side of the road with a shot gun house built for saw mill workers on either side. The hotel faced mostly north but with just a hint of east. If a crow flew off the front porch and didn't veer from its course it would end up in Memphis, Tennessee, instead of Missouri, which is where due north would take it. Painted pristine white with a wide front porch held up with square pillars and a banister between them, it looked more like an old plantation home than a hotel. A hitching rail divided the parking area from the front lawn, lush and green. Flower beds had recently been set out with lantana, petunias, marigolds and rose moss. On one side of the building Quincy could see rose bushes that had been recently transplanted, trimmed back and prepared for summer growth. On the other side, the earth had been dug up and a small wisteria and larger lilac bush hugged the house.

Nothing got past Quincy Massey, not a single overturned dirt clod. With a trained eye for deception he studied the three women on the porch of the small hotel. They looked innocent as newborn lambs, but Ralph Contiello had gone missing and someone was to blame. One of those red heads had been his wife and the trio had been the last to actually talk to him. Innocent looking did not mean sin free.

Oscar Pendergraft was the sheriff of Union County, Arkansas and he was in complete disagreement with Quincy Massey. "You ain't goin' to find nothing here. Those ladies couldn't kill nobody and that Contiello was a skunk. He's most likely run off with another woman to beat on and humiliate. I don't hold to women not takin' their marriage vows serious, but I dang sure don't think a man ought to beat his wife, neither. He had a temper, that man did, and he chased everything that wore a skirt. Could be that he's somewhere at the bottom of the river or buried in a shallow grave because he flirted with the wrong man's wife. But I'll bet you the O'Shea sisters

8

didn't have a dang thing to do with it."

Patrick O'Shea was a stout man with a receding hair line and Oscar had spent many hours drinking coffee with him in the Black Swan dining room. They'd discussed politics, crops and business on more than one occasion and he'd sorely missed his old friend when the cursed flu took him six months ago. Oscar would never believe one of Patrick's daughters would be capable of anything illegal, most especially murder. Even if that rascal Ralph did deserve it, not a one of them could kill him. If homicide had been possible or legal, Ralph would have been dead months ago, the first time Catherine found out he was beating on her younger sister.

"I've seen it all and nothing surprises me," Quincy said.

"Well, it would dang sure surprise me. Patrick come here and built the Black Swan back when they was putting a town together for the saw mill men's families. Even before the Commerical Hotel was built. He raised those girls right and ain't none of them a killer. If any of them had a thing to do with Ralph's disappearance I'd eat my dirty socks for supper," Oscar argued.

They opened the doors to the sheriff's car, a Buick Roadster. Granted it was three years old, but it was still shiny new because Oscar kept it clean as it had been the day it was delivered to his office in El Dorado, the seat of Union County. He shook the legs of his khaki colored trousers down over shiny black shoes. He sucked in his gut so it didn't hang out over his belt quite so badly, and smiled at the ladies having their afternoon tea on the porch.

Quincy wore a black three-pieced suit, all the buttons fastened on the jacket and the vest. A black silk four-in-hand no-nonsense tie was knotted at the throat of a crisp white shirt. Straight legged trousers ended at the tops of highly polished boots. He wore his hat with the front brim tilted down shading dark brown eyes set below thick, black eyebrows. Standing tall at six feet three inches, his angular face bore a serious expression. Everything about Quincy spelled dangerous except his full mouth which gave him just a hint of vulnerability.

Oscar tipped his hat. "Mornin' ladies. How ya'll doin' this fine afternoon?"

"Good morning, Oscar," Catherine said. "What brings you to town this fine spring day?"

And is that the devil in disguise you've brought to our porch?

Oscar leaned against a porch post. "Ya'll

10

opened up the Black Swan for business again?"

"Just today. We've been doing spring cleaning to keep our minds busy and off Momma's passing," Catherine said.

"She'll be sorely missed. That Ella O'Shea was a fine woman," Oscar said.

Catherine picked up a plate of cookies and held them out toward the two men. "Thank you, sir, and what can we do for you? A cup of tea and cookies? Alice made them just this morning. We can rustle up some more cups."

"No, ma'am, I've got ya'll a customer. This would be Quincy Massey from up in Little Rock. He's a detective who's been hired to look into the disappearance of Ralph Contiello. He needs a place to stay and wants to go over all that again with you ladies. He'll be spending a few days here in Huttig while he questions a lot of folks, so don't ya'll let it worry you none. It ain't just you all's story he's looking into." Oscar's tone was apologetic.

He pointed as he introduced the sisters. "This would be Catherine, the oldest of the ladies. This is Alice, the middle daughter. And this is Bridget; she'd be Ralph's wife."

Quincy tipped his hat but didn't say anything. Catherine was the one who'd bear

11

watching. Her eyes held his with no fear; few men could do that. Until that moment he'd never met a woman who wouldn't back down from his glare. Alice stared at him as if she were studying a frog in a swamp, a blank look on her face and in her eyes. He wouldn't be surprised if she was a little touched. Bridget wouldn't look at him at all.

"But we told it to *you* two weeks ago, Oscar. Why would we have to go over it again? Have they found Ralph?" Bridget asked.

"No, that's why Mr. Massey has been brought in on the deal. Ralph's family wants some solid answers. Guess I would too if my son was missing but I done told the detective here that you ladies had nothing to do with the man's disappearance," Oscar said.

"Are you a Pinkerton man? I thought they settled labor disputes and strikes. Didn't know they'd be out investigating a sorry excuse of a man gone missing." Catherine sipped her tea as if she'd just told the man she liked his tie rather than insulting him.

Quincy didn't answer. He'd been insulted by experts. Catherine O'Shea was an amateur, even if a brazen one. He was there to do a job and getting riled right off the bat wasn't the way to get it done.

All of them were red haired, but then he'd expected that when he read the report. The name O'Shea didn't leave much doubt about their heritage. What he hadn't expected was the beauty. Catherine had the darkest hair, the burgundy of a sugar maple leaf in the fall. Big olive green eyes were set in a face that belied red haired women's nature. There wasn't a freckle to be seen. Her oval face had a strong chin that said she'd take little or no sass from anyone and her lips were made for kissing.

Alice probably had been described as a carrot top when she was a child. Her hair had darkened somewhat with age but still wasn't nearly as dark or burgundy as Catherine's. She had a few freckles strewn haphazardly across her pert turned up nose and her mouth wasn't nearly as full. She chewed on her lower lip nervously and looked anywhere but at him. Quincy could break her in less than an hour. If they knew where Contiello was, it would be Alice who'd give the secret away.

Bridget was the pretty one. Strawberry blond hair, green eyes so light they were practically transparent aqua, short of stature, feminine. But fidgety, almost jumpy as she sipped tea from a china cup.

13

"So why don't you stay at the Commercial Hotel? That's where Oscar found Ralph's car when he disappeared," Catherine asked.

"I like something a little smaller and the good sheriff here has vouched for the food in the Black Swan," Quincy said.

Catherine stood up. "Then we will be delighted to have a paying customer. Bring your bags and I'll show you to a room. Would you like the one nearest to the bathroom? It has its advantages. But then when the hotel fills up, you'll be kept awake if someone is up and down all night long."

Without a word, he returned to the car for his baggage. This would be a three day job at the most then he could catch the train back to Little Rock. He removed a suitcase and a briefcase from the back seat and carried them to the front porch.

The ladies might all be easy on the eyes but he wasn't as impressed as Oscar had been when he talked about the O'Shea girls. Quincy didn't cotton to women in pants, even if the war had altered social rules, and all three sisters wore those new fangled women's overalls. Granted they wore them well and had feminized them with white blouses and straw hats with satin ribbon bands to keep the sun off their faces, but women were supposed to wear dresses not

14

pants. Even if they were blousy, they had legs and were gathered tight at the ankle, making them glorified pants. Women who wore them were asking for trouble letting men look at their bare ankles. The only thing he despised worse than women in the flowing overalls were those who'd started wearing leggings for anything other than riding a horse. Even then they looked better in a split skirt riding habit. Or the new skirt length ending at mid-calf when they should be dragging the ground.

"I'll show you to your room. Have you had dinner? In this part of the world we usually call our mid-day meal dinner and the evening one is supper," Catherine said in a slow southern drawl.

"Yes, but you do serve supper here at the hotel, don't you?"

Catherine led the way inside. "At five o'clock. It'll be slow for a few days until word gets around we've reopened after Momma's passing. That should give you time to do a little investigating before supper."

The lobby wasn't huge but looked comfortable with the bright yellow wallpaper, three separate seating groups and fireplace with rocking chairs in a semi-circle in front of it. A small blaze warmed the room, inviting patrons to sit a spell and have a visit. Before he could take in the whole scene she motioned him toward a solid oak stair case leading up to the bedrooms. Polished to a gleam, the banisters, steps and railing matched the shiny floor in the lobby.

"When did your mother die?" he asked.

Catherine's green eyes flashed. "If you are worth your salt as a detective, you already know that, sir. I'm sure Oscar has filled you in or else you have an actual report from the Contiello family about the events surrounding the disappearance of their son."

"I do, but I'd like to hear it all from each of you, individually."

She opened the door to the first room on the left, determined to make him miserable. His room would be subject to the noise of other guests stomping up and down the stairs. Maybe after a few sleepless nights he'd give up and check into the Commercial.

"Is this room satisfactory?"

"It's fine," he said. Actually it was very nice. Full sized bed with a nice piece work quilt spread tightly on top; washstand with white towels stacked on the top; shaving chest with a small bowl and pitcher set, plus a little swivel mirror he could tilt just right in the mornings; rocking chair next to the window overlooking the front lawn; and crisp white curtains billowing into the room with the March breeze.

"Good. You can join us at supper in a couple of hours. We'll be glad to answer any questions you have," Catherine said.

"I want to talk to you individually," he said, again.

"What you want, Pinky, and what you get are two different things."

She inhaled deeply when she reached the bottom of the stairs but she didn't stop. She opened the door and put her finger over her lips to hush any talk from Bridget or Alice. The window right above the porch roof was open and Quincy would have his ear hanging out like bed sheets on the line on wash day morning if he was a good detective and she didn't see the Contiellos hiring anything but the very best.

"Act normal," she mouthed.

They both nodded nervously.

"I'm glad I put a ham in the oven since we will definitely be feeding more than family tonight," Alice said.

"Think I should make a coconut pie?" Bridget picked up on the conversation but still attempted to murder her handkerchief. There wouldn't be anything left of it but a few frazzled strands of cotton if she didn't stop the constant twisting.

"That would be nice. I'll make biscuits and candied yams. Momma always said a ham had to have yams to make it worth eating," Catherine said.

As if on cue, they went silent remembering their mother, Ella O'Shea. She'd given them their names because Catherine meant earth; Alice, air; and Bridget, water. She'd told them when they were little girls that they could conquer the world as long as they stood together. The O'Shea name meant dauntless or steadfast and she fully well expected them to live up to it even if they were women. The O'Sheas were proud Irish and their symbol was the black swan inside a perfect circle with its wings uplifted, just like the emblem on the sign swinging from a chain in the front yard.

They sipped lukewarm tea in silence. Last fall, when the flu epidemic swept through southern Arkansas, they'd lost their father, Patrick. One of the first to die in Huttig, they'd buried him in the Harper Springs Cemetery less than two miles from the Black Swan hotel. Ella had literally held her breath in fear one of her daughters would contract the dreaded disease. Neighbors dropped; the cemetery had more and more new graves; the mortician's bank account grew. Finally, after six months, the funerals slowed down and life went back to normal. Everyone breathed a sigh of relief, then old Granny Oldham took sick and Ella took her a quart of soup before she'd been diagnosed. Ella came down with the flu within days after Granny Oldham was buried. A week later she was dead.

They'd closed up the hotel for three weeks at the doctor's recommendation. Now it was open again and the first visitor was going to be poking his nose into their business. Well, he'd have the answers they wanted to give and not another thing. Bridget was still fragile, like water. Alice had air for brains. Catherine had learned to live with disappointments and besides she was the earth. Solid. Dependable. She'd take care of her sisters.

"Shall we go inside?" Catherine asked.

Bridget nodded and picked up the tray with the china tea set, cups and matching saucers. Alice gathered up the white linen napkins and cookie platter.

The Black Swan was sixteen years old that spring. It had been built back in 1903, a year after Huttig came into being. Home of one of the largest sawmills in the area, the town was formed to provide mill workers a place to live. Men had brought families and that created a need for a school, churches, banks, hotels and stores. Huttig had been built to satisfy that need. Patrick O'Shea had a wife and three daughters and managed a fairly large hotel in Hope, Arkansas. He'd saved a little money and heard what was going on near the Louisiana border so he brought his family to Huttig and put up the first hotel in town. The Commercial Hotel had been built not long afterward and drew most of the company business as did the Company store, but Patrick had always run a clean hotel. The food was good. A reputation had been built. The Black Swan's registers showed many repeat customers.

The front door opened into a small lobby with settees forming three seating areas. Ashtrays were available on the end tables to keep smokers' ashes off Ella's wool rugs. Along the back wall was a counter where Patrick had conducted business for fourteen years. A guest register rested on a swivel stand, an ink pen and well waited for signatures. Cubby holes for mail or messages were built into the wall behind the pine wood counter, and a money box was hidden in a locked drawer. A huge stone fireplace, like those in Ireland, according to Patrick, covered one wall and in the winter months it was ablaze most days. Folks said the fireplace and half dozen rocking chairs surrounding it brought them to the Black Swan as much as the ambience and the good food.

A large, square archway with gingerbread trim in the corners led into a dining room which could seat as many as twenty four at a time. It wasn't unusual for it to be filled and more people in the lobby waiting for a place to sit. Four high backed cane bottom chairs surrounded each table covered with a white table cloth. Fresh cut flowers from Ella's flower beds often graced the middle of each table. Napkins were always folded like a swan and Alice's framed oil paintings decorated the brightly papered walls.

Toward the back of the dining room stood a six foot sideboard with a French beveled oval mirror set in the middle of the upper part. A shelf above the mirror displayed Ella's special lead glass collection. The table top below held more of her fancy crystal and the drawers and doors below stored dozens of white linen napkins. Right behind the sideboard, a doorway opened into the kitchen where the newest and best appliances were standing at the ready. One of the newest inventions was the most prized thing in the house, a refrigerator; the generator to run the thing had to be housed in the basement but the ladies no longer even heard the noisy thing.

The next best thing in the hotel was indoor plumbing. Patrick had insisted the year before he died that they get modernized. They had converted part of the hallway into a bathroom, and put one in their housing quarters as well. Alice said she felt like she'd died and gone to heaven that first winter she didn't have to make runs down to the outhouse. The three girls were elated to be among the first people in Huttig to have an inside bathroom even if it was because they lived in a hotel.

To the left of the front door, stairs led up to the rooms. There were eight small bedrooms, four on each side of the hallway. Spotlessly clean and offering most of the comforts of home, they were seldom empty. From the back side of the lobby a doorway led into the family's private quarters: a living room and two bedrooms. Ella had declared when the place was built that it would be foolish to have two kitchens. She'd be cooking and the family could take their meals in the dining room. She'd also decided that separate bedrooms for her daughters weren't necessary. Living together would teach them sharing. One big room: three full sized identical beds ordered from the Sears catalog just like everything else in the hotel: three oak dressers to match the six foot beds which looked enormous when three little bitty girls first slept in them: three stuffed chairs for comfortable reading or playing with doll babies: three lamps and a complete wall of books that had gone from children's reading material to grown women's altogether too fast.

Bridget was three the year they came to Huttig. Alice, four. Catherine, five. Patrick had never said a word about a house full of daughters but sometimes when he took her fishing, Catherine wondered if he'd liked to have had at least one son.

After they deposited the tea service and leftover cookies in the kitchen, Catherine led the way back through the dining room and lobby into their private quarters. She shut the door firmly and leaned against it.

"What are we going to do?" Bridget whispered. She was as pale as a freshly bleached dish towel and still terrified that Ralph's disappearance would be blamed on her.

"We're going to remain calm and answer his questions but not alone. Never, ever alone. If he can get us by ourselves he'll try to pry information from us or set us against one another. So we'll answer what ever he wants but only while we are together,"

Catherine said. "Other than that, he's a paying customer and we'll treat him as such."

"I'm scared," Bridget said.

Catherine hugged her youngest sister. "Don't be. It's over. Finished. Done with. We will stand together and nothing can break a three fold cord. Remember, Momma said that."

"I don't know if I can sit at the table with him," Alice said.

"Oh, yes you can and we will since he's our only guest. We're having supper family style so no one has to go to the kitchen for seconds or to refill a tea glass. Just be careful not to let him catch any of us alone. We can do anything together," Catherine said.

Bridget still worried the hanky. "But if I told the truth?"

"You did tell the truth. Now hush. It's time you started that pie. It'll keep your hands busy and you mind off old Pinky up there."

Bridget giggled. "He looks more like a blacky than a pinky."

"Or the devil himself," Alice said.

"You are both right and we'll send him home dehorned with his tail between his legs," Catherine told them.

Bridget stopped tearing up a perfectly good handkerchief and Alice actually smiled. They trooped out and into the kitchen.

Catherine peeled sweet potatoes and hoped she could keep her sisters from saying too much. Both tended to over compensate with words when they were nervous.

Ella had often said of all the girls she'd given her third daughter the right name. Bridget was as unstable as water and Ella hoped she'd be happy when she married Ralph Contiello from El Dorado. She'd thought her daughter was making a good match; as good as could be expected if the groom wasn't Irish. Dark haired and good looking, Ralph appeared to adore Bridget in the courting process. It wasn't until they'd been married a month that Bridget confided in Catherine about the beatings and his temper. That was a year ago. Next week Bridget was filing for divorce. By the spring of 1919 women had come a long way in their battle for rights but it was going to create a stink that could be smelled all the way to the Atlantic Ocean when Bridget filed against Ralph on the grounds of desertion.

Alice was as flighty as air, changing direction on a whim. It had been said when she was younger that she wasn't really right in the head, and Catherine had gone to battle many times to discredit that horrid lie. It wasn't that she lacked intelligence; it was simply that she marched to a very different drummer.

Quincy unpacked and sat quietly in the rocking chair. Their voices filtered up through the window and into his room. Everything was too normal and that made him wonder just what had happened when Ralph left El Dorado in a snit to bring his wife home a month ago. He'd find out; he didn't have open cases. When he was put on a job, the case was closed permanently when he went home.

He'd seen defiance in Catherine's eyes so he'd use the soft approach at supper. Get them all good and comfortable and then spring a few well placed questions that would tell the tale. He'd interviewed women secret agents and spies in his time overseas with the war effort. The O'Shea ladies could not hide a thing from him.

CHAPTER TWO

The sun was still fairly high in the sky when Quincy brushed his black hair back with his fingertips and slipped into the suit coat he'd hung carefully over the back of a straight back chair. He'd reread the report the sheriff had given him so he was very familiar with what the O'Shea women had already said. However there were more details; he could feel it in his bones and they never lied to him.

Catherine looked up at him from the bottom of the stairs. "Would you join us at our table? We don't often have only one guest so we have set supper up family style."

The transformation was amazing. She'd removed those abominable overalls and dressed like a woman. Her hair had been pinned high on her head and he'd not realized how tall she was. When he reached the last step he could have kissed her without having to bend very far. Of course, kissing Catherine was the last thing on his mind.

He shook his head to dislodge the vision of her in his arms.

"Is there a reason you want to eat alone?" Catherine's tone was edgy and crisp.

"I'm sorry. I wasn't saying no to your invitation. I felt a gnat on my eyelashes. I would be honored to have dinner with you all." Quincy was more than pleased to agree since that would give him time to talk to them. The whole story could be revealed over a nice supper. It was possible he'd have enough evidence for an arrest by morning because he was sure more had happened than had been written up in that scant report in his room.

She led him to a table laden with sliced ham, sweet potatoes, green beans with bacon bits floating in them, biscuits and a huge bowl of mashed potatoes. "Please sit right there." She pointed at a place with good china plates, matching serviceable silver flatware and a napkin folded like a swan with its wings uplifted.

"This looks wonderful." A little honey might net him a few flies.

"Thank you. Momma insisted on a pretty table," Alice said.

They'd all three dressed for the evening

28

meal. Tailored skirts. Navy serge for Catherine topped with a crisp white blouse with a lace collar. Green and ivory plaid for Alice with an ecru blouse with a dark green satin bow around the neck. Black for Bridget with deep pockets decorated with buttons, topped with a middy blouse with a red tie. Not really what he'd expected from women in mourning but at least it beat those horrid overalls.

They passed bowls and platters and chattered amongst themselves about their mother's recipes. Again, almost too normal.

"So you were all quite close to your mother?" He asked.

"Like sisters," Alice said. "She was our dear friend."

Quincy raised an eyebrow.

"You're wondering why we aren't wearing black from head to toe and taken to our beds, since we were very close to our parents, aren't you?" Catherine asked.

"The thought crossed my mind," he answered.

"Momma made us promise before she died that we wouldn't waste time carryin' on like a bunch of half-wits. She said we could wear black to the funeral and we could cry. It was normal to weep but afterward we were to get on with life. No black.

No going to bed for a year," Alice said.

"She knew she was dying?" Quincy asked.

"How many folks do you know who lived through the flu?" Bridget asked.

"Not many."

"Soon as Bridget arrived that morning she called us to her bedside and gave us our orders and her blessings. She hung on until we were all three here," Alice said.

"So you came from El Dorado before your mother passed?" Quincy bit into the best ham he'd ever eaten, and whichever sister had said ham was meant to be served with sweetened yams had surely known her facts.

"Of course. Catherine called me on the telephone. Momma loved the modern re-rigerator and the indoor plumbing but she always said telephones were a nuisance. Just a means of spreading gossip. It was Daddy who insisted we have one in the hotel for business reasons. We had one in our house because Ralph had everything. A new automobile every single year and indoor plumbing and everything money could buy. So Catherine called and I caught the next train this way," Bridget rattled on.

"Why didn't Ralph bring you?"

"Because he said I couldn't come. He was afraid I'd get the flu, and besides, he liked to have his way."

So far, so good, Catherine thought. *Give him so many facts he'll bog down in them.*

"And you disobeyed him?" Quincy asked.

"My mother was on her death bed and I wanted to tell her good-bye. What would you have done, Mr. Massey?"

"I'm just trying to get a picture of what happened. I'm not passing judgment."

"Good, because if you are any kind of son, you'd be there when your momma calls for you. As it was, I only got here a few hours before she died. We had the funeral the very next day."

Catherine bit her lip to keep from grinning. Bridget was holding her own and turning the tables on the smooth talking detective.

"And it was after the funeral that Ralph showed up here?"

Alice laid her fork down. "Yes, it was. He came through the front door after supper time like a bull in a grocery store. Bellowing about Bridget disobeying him. The two of us were upstairs cleaning rooms. The doctor said everything had to be washed down and we had to close the doors for three weeks. I came out of the room I was working on and Bridget did the same. She was scared to death of that man, let me tell you. He was evil and he beat her every time he could figure out a reason to jerk his belt off."

Bridget picked up the story line. "I thought he loved me when he was courtin' me but I found out pretty quick that sweet, smooth talking gentleman wasn't the man I married. I knew he'd be horrible but I had to see my Momma and tell her good-bye. Momma always kept a little two shot gun in her dresser drawer so after the funeral I went in there and put it in my pocket. I'd decided I wasn't going back with him and maybe a gun would scare him into leaving me alone. I can show it to you after supper. I put it back in the dresser drawer. Anyway, we were at the top of the stairs and he grabbed my shoulders and started shaking me. The things he said don't bear repeating. What he called me wouldn't be fit for mixed company. I jerked that gun out of my pocket and pointed it at him. That shut him up for a minute, then he started unbuckling his belt telling me I didn't have the brains or the nerve to shoot him and if I did his parents would see to it I was as dead as he was. I figured that wouldn't be as bad as living with him so I pulled the trigger. The bullet went past him and stuck in the wall. I'm not much of a shot. I should've given the gun to Catherine. She can shoot the eyes out of a water moccasin at twenty yards. I think Daddy wanted a son and he taught Catherine things most boys know. Like fishing and shooting and how to skin a squirrel."

"That's when I started screaming at him to get out of our home," Alice said. "He didn't waste any time getting to the bottom of the stairs, let me tell you. Besides, Catherine had come out of the kitchen and he's afraid of her."

"Is or was?" Quincy asked.

"Who knows? If he's alive then the next time he comes in this house I won't miss. Momma's gun has two barrels. I'm still wondering why Bridget didn't cock the hammer and give it another try. She might have missed the first time but her aim might have been better if she wasn't shaking like a leaf. I won't miss if I'm the one holding that gun. If he's pushin' up daisies then good riddance, and may his soul rot in hell. Pass the biscuits please, Bridget," Catherine said.

"Did you kill him?" Quincy looked straight at Catherine.

"I did not kill that man but I will if he ever shows his face on our property again. Bridget has seen a lawyer and there will be a divorce. It will take time because the courts aren't too sympathetic to woman

33

leaving her husband but Ralph hasn't been seen or heard since that night. I think that is desertion." Catherine's eyes never faltered.

"Why not file on abuse charges?" Quincy asked.

"Because I promised to obey him and a jury of men would say that he had the right to beat me when I didn't," Bridget answered.

Quincy turned his icy glare to Bridget. "Did you kill him?"

"No, but if he comes back I'll try again," she said.

"And before you ask, neither did I," Alice said bluntly.

"So you shot at him and he left?"

"That's what happened. You want to see the bullet. Catherine dug it out of the woodwork and we patched up the hole. But we still got the bullet. You're welcome to look at it and the gun. The Sheriff examined both of them," Bridget said.

"Yes, I would like that later," Quincy said.

"Any more questions?" Catherine asked.

"A couple. Why did you marry him?"

"Because we thought he was a good man and I thought I loved him. Momma named us after the elements. Catherine is named for the earth and she's got the good common sense in the family. Alice is named after air and she goes around with her head in the clouds. I'm named after water and I'm not real stable when it comes to affairs of the heart. I was in love with Billy Mack Talley when I was sixteen and we were going to elope. The next morning I woke up and decided I didn't love him. I just wanted to be married. He was as flighty as I am and before the day was out he was walking about town with Martha Mae Greenbury. Anyway, Ralph seemed to be a good solid man and he was older and he kept telling me how much he loved me and I thought he was stable and he'd make a good husband."

"How much older?"

"Ten years. I was eighteen last year when we married. I'm nineteen now. He was twenty nine on his last birthday," Bridget said.

They were telling the truth, he'd bet his future on it, but he'd bet his life they weren't telling the whole truth. Something else happened that night. He must've come back and Catherine had control of the gun that time.

"So after he left the Black Swan that night after your mother's funeral, you never saw him again?" Quincy asked.

"After that night none of us has seen

him," Catherine said.

Alice had enough of answering questions and had a few of her own to ask Mr. Massey. "Why did the sheriff bring you down here? Why didn't you drive your own vehicle?"

"I don't own an automobile. I'm not home enough to warrant buying one. I traveled to El Dorado on the train, talked to Ralph's family to get their side of the story, and would've come here the same way but the good sheriff offered to drive me since he had other business in the area."

"So are you going to walk all over town gathering this information?" Alice asked.

"I suppose I am," Quincy said.

"We own a Ford and you're welcome to drive it. That way you can get your business done twice as fast. Please pass the green beans. It won't be long now until we plant the garden. I love the first new potatoes and green beans that come out of the garden. We dug it up a few weeks ago and got the dirt ready. We've bought onion slips but we haven't had time to get them planted. But in this part of the world we have nice weather all the way to winter and always get two crops so it don't matter if we're a little late getting them planted," Alice said.

Catherine nodded in agreement.

Bridget held her hands tightly in her lap

to keep from shuddering. She just hoped they'd cleaned the car well enough to offer to a big city detective. Was there something still in it that would tell him what really happened that night?

"Thank you ladies. I appreciate the offer of your automobile. Do you think I could borrow it after supper? I'd like to visit the Commercial Hotel. Those folks would actually be the last people who saw Ralph, wouldn't they?"

"That's what the sheriff told us when he came around a couple of days after Momma's funeral. He said Ralph went back to the hotel in his car, went to his room and was never seen again. I'd be willing to bet he went to a bar, got drunk on bootleg whiskey and went home with some other woman," Bridget said.

"But you'll have to talk to them to get their story. We haven't been out and about much these past few weeks. We've only been to the Company store for supplies. We've been in semi-quarantine. No one in Huttig wants another outbreak of the flu so folks have avoided us. There were barely a dozen at Momma's funeral," Catherine said.

Quincy nodded. Yes, indeed he would like to have the advantage of a car and would go to the Commercial right after he'd finished dessert. Wasn't one of them talking about a coconut pie? He shut his eyes and listened to them talking about the weather and roses and gardening. Catherine had the deepest voice. Smooth, yes, but the honey was tempered with a shot of moonshine. Alice had a thin voice with a slight nasal twang. Bridget spoke softly. It had been her voice that had drifted up from the porch saying she was making pie.

After they finished dessert and coffee, he drove to the Commercial. It was a big square hotel with a porch all around the bottom and a balcony around the top. Second floor rooms had doors that opened out onto the continuous balcony so the people could come and go without using the lobby. He sat in the Ford and studied the hotel. Ralph had had a second floor room according to the report and he'd used the back stairs when he came back from the Black Swan. Too bad the hotel wasn't self contained. More people would have seen him.

They left the dishes and food on the table and went to their bedroom and all three fell across one bed, lacing their fingers together.

"Do you think he believed us?" Bridget asked.

"Sure he did but he's like a hound with a ham bone. He's going to gnaw at it a while before he leaves us in peace." Catherine sat up, a sister on either side of her.

"What are we going to do?" Alice asked.

"You both did very well tonight, I'm not worried. We just have to stick to our story and never waver from it. Answer his questions. He'll most likely ask them a hundred times over again just to see if he can trip us up. But for now, we've got to put away the food. No use in owning a fancy ice box if we don't use the thing," Catherine said.

"Did you think he was handsome?" Bridget asked.

"A woman would be blind if she didn't. It's why they sent him. To catch us off guard," Catherine answered. "But he's surely not my type. He's too cocky and sure of himself to suit me."

Quincy introduced himself to the night clerk. "The sheriff said he'd come by and tell you I was investigating the disappearance of Ralph Contiello. Were you on duty the night Mr. Contiello went missing?" He asked.

"Yes, sir. Right here. He come in late that evening and rented a room. I could tell he was mad by the way he was talking."

Quincy leaned on the counter. "And how was that?"

"When I asked him how many nights he needed the room, he said that he'd only need it one night and for me not to come around poking my nose in his business if I heard a bunch of wailing coming out of the room."

"Why would he say that?"

"I reckon he was plenty mad because Miz Bridget come down here to see her Momma before she passed on. Folks in town said he whipped her awful when she didn't mind him. They say that's what happens when a girl marries a feller she don't really know. Mothers around here have got to using that to put the fear of God into young girls who want to step out with big city boys. Anyway, he said he'd be back in a while and he tore out of here in that automobile sitting right out there."

"How long was it between the time he left and he returned? Was he still mad when he got back? Did Bridget come with him?" Quincy deliberately asked a barrage of questions.

"It wasn't more than half an hour. Don't know if he was mad or not but nobody was with him. He parked out there under the pines and went up the side steps to his

40

room. He had one on the top floor. I saw him come slinking in all by hisself and figured things hadn't gone like he wanted them. There was a man in the room next to him that told the sheriff he heard him prowling around a few minutes before he left again. I didn't know nothing about that because wherever he went he didn't drive his car. It's still sittin' in the same spot out there. Bridget don't want the thing and his parents haven't come to claim it yet. Guess they're hopin' he's off on a lark of some kind and it'll be there for him when he gets back. You ask me, Ralph Contiello ain't comin' back. You want to look at it? It's sure a pretty thing. Buick Roadster with every extra thing they could put on it."

"That would be a big help. And the room?"

"Oh, it wasn't even touched. Bed wasn't unmade. Towel was still clean so we just gathered up his suitcase and we'll be keeping it 'til his folks come get it. Want to look at it?"

Quincy nodded and the clerk brought it from under the counter, flipped the locks and opened it up. "One change of clothing and shaving equipment."

"Thank you. Has anyone else been in his automobile since he left it there?"

"No sir. It was locked up tight and the sheriff said I wasn't to let nobody near it. Key was is in that suitcase right there. In the side pocket. It's in the safe now. Sheriff thought it would be best to do that. He came by this afternoon and said it was all right for you to look in there but no one else. Said you was a real detective. Is that the truth?"

"Yes, it is. I've been hired by the Contiello family to either find their son or discover what happened to him. You want to venture a guess?"

"I been studyin' on it for weeks. I reckon he met up with his match when he went over there to the Black Swan. I wouldn't tangle with Catherine for no amount of money and Alice, well, she's odd, you know. She's liable to do most anything and not even remember it the next day. Bridget had them to back her up so he didn't stand no chance of gettin' her out of there if she didn't want to go and what woman would want to go home to a whoopin'? So he came back here and thought about it and then went back on foot to sneak in and try to talk sense to his wife. Whatever happened, it happened at the Black Swan. I reckon they killed him and buried his body somewhere over there on the property. That Catherine could've done it and not batted an eye. Alice could have stabbed him and had a cup of tea while she watched him die. Bridget sure could have finished him off to keep from takin' another beatin' from him. Can't say I'd blame any one of the three but I guess the law would have a different idea about that."

"I see," Quincy said. "I'll come around tomorrow and have a look at that car in the daylight. What time are you working?"

"I start my shift at four o'clock. The key is in the safe if you get here before that. I'll leave a note that the sheriff said you was to be allowed to have it."

"Thank you again." Quincy left by the front door. Tomorrow he would have a long look at both cars: the O'Sheas' and Ralph's. The story might be told right there but the clerk could be right. Ralph went out again and where else could he have been going? He'd driven from El Dorado to get his wife and had no other business in town. Or did he? Had he gone into a bar for a drink and left with someone else like Bridget said? The case surely wasn't solved just yet.

The ladies were sitting in the lobby when he returned. Catherine had a book in her hands. Alice had set up an easel and was painting. Bridget was knitting something in pink.

Catherine looked up. "Find anything helpful?"

"Not yet, but I will. Did I notice a garden out in your back yard when I took an afternoon stroll?"

"Of course. Momma had to have her garden and flowers. It was a sight getting all those pine trees cleared those first few years so she could plant a garden. Daddy finally got enough trees out that it gets some sun. We grow our own vegetables for the hotel from spring until fall," Alice said.

Catherine cocked her head to one side. "We just recently dug it up and it's rained this week so it's a bit muddy. Why do you ask?"

"Just wondering. And I suppose you transplanted rose and lilac bushes recently, also?"

"We sure did. The lilac bush went to the side yard and the rose bush that was there wasn't getting enough light so we brought it to the other side. You'd never believe how much we have to do to keep them happy."

Quincy sighed. Three days could turn into a week or maybe two. He was glad he'd packed old clothing with his field kit.

"You ladies ever heard of fingerprints?"

44

"I read an article about that a few years ago. Something about making a person put their fingertips in ink and then put them on paper. It said they used it in Leavenworth Federal Prison," Catherine said.

"That's right. I've brought a kit to take prints from inside your automobile and Ralph's. Would you be willing to let me take your prints?"

"Whatever you need," Catherine said.

Bridget dropped the pink knitting in her lap. "But I've been inside Ralph's car many times."

"I realize that so we'll know that the ones on the passenger's side are yours. Either of you other two left prints in the car?" He asked. Lord, he hated the thought of digging up a whole garden searching for a body.

"Not me. I wouldn't ride with that fool for all the dirt in Arkansas," Catherine said.

"Don't look at me. I wouldn't leave prints in his car, either," Alice said.

"Could we take your prints right now?" He asked.

"How do you get the ink off?" Alice asked.

"Same way you clean your hands after you paint," Quincy answered.

"Well, they're already dirty so it would make sense. Yes, of course, go get the stuff and we'll get it over with. Then maybe you can go home."

"Alice, we mustn't be rude," Bridget said.

"I wasn't rude. I was stating facts."

Quincy brought his kit into the lobby and set up shop on the counter. First he printed Bridget. Eight fingers and two thumbs. Almost child sized. Maybe if she'd been as big as Catherine, Ralph would have thought twice before he whipped her. Then Alice, and finally Catherine.

When he touched her forefinger, pressing it onto the ink saturated felt pad to the cardboard a shock glued him to the floor. He was suddenly tongue tied with the effects of the bolt. He didn't like the Irish lady. As a matter of fact, he really, really didn't like her. She was everything he disliked in a woman. Too strong. Too opinionated. Too independent. Too tall. Red hair. Not one thing about her appealed to him.

There was no way in God's great green earth he was going to even spend one minute admitting he was physically attracted to her. He liked short little blond women with big, innocent blue eyes like Elizabeth. Besides he was a fine detective and married to his job. He had no time for women.

Catherine wasn't prepared for the jolt of

his fingers touching hers. Not even Ira had caused a sensation like that in the pit of her stomach and she'd been engaged to him. She managed to keep her emotions tied down firmly and didn't give him the satisfaction of knowing how his touch had affected her. That's all she needed, a heart whining after the very worst man in the whole world for her.

CHAPTER THREE

The next morning Quincy ate alone in the dining room. He ordered two fried eggs, bacon, biscuits, gravy and a cinnamon raisin muffin. Bridget took his order. Alice brought it out to him. The women ignored him as they wandered in and out of the kitchen talking about the menu for Tuesday. Should they go ahead with the old menus or update them? After enough words to make his ears ache they decided to keep the old one. He looked forward to a couple of interviews where he asked a simple question and got a direct one-line answer.

Like the sheriff promised, the food was excellent at the Black Swan. And if he'd filtered through the conversation properly then pot roast, hot yeast rolls, chocolate pie, and pound cake topped with canned peaches was served on Tuesday. Hopefully the dining room would be full; there was no better place to hide or to ferret out information than in a group of people who were familiar with each other.

He ate fast and got out. That morning he would talk to the neighbors. After lunch, he'd go over the O'Sheas' automobile with a magnifying glass and fingerprint dust. He'd do the same to Ralph's automobile after supper. Hopefully he wouldn't have to actually hunt up a shovel.

He knocked on the door of a white frame house built like many of the homes in Huttig. Basic housing for company families: shotgun if it had one bedroom with a living room right inside the front door, a kitchen behind that and a bedroom on past the kitchen. Square if it was a two bedroom abode; living room inside the front door, kitchen straight ahead, a bedroom off each room. Mr. and Mrs. Matthis had a two bedroom and were among those who'd made improvements. They had a porch extending the length of the front of the house and wrapping far enough around the side so someone could come out the kitchen door onto it. The flower beds around the porch were yellow with jonquils, flower pots were set on every porch step and ferns hung between the porch posts.

The door swung open and a chubby lady in a floral cotton dress stood there with a big smile on her face. "Hello, are you the Pinkerton man? I've been expecting you'd want to talk to us. I'm Mabel Matthis and my husband is Henry. Come in. We'll have coffee and cookies in the living room. Henry is waiting for you."

He removed his hat and followed her. "Thank you."

The other part of the team who'd been expecting him rose from a chair and extended his hand. "I'm Henry Matthis. We'll be glad to help any way we can."

"Just settle yourself in one of those chairs and get comfortable. I'll just be a minute gettin' something from the kitchen," she said.

"So how long you goin' to look into this business of Ralph's bein' missin'?" Henry asked.

"Until I get it solved or find him," Quincy said.

Mabel brought a tray with a fancy silver coffee service, three fine bone China cups and saucers, and a plate of sugar cookies.

"Are you really one of them Pinkerton men, Mr. Massey?" Mrs. Matthis asked.

"No, ma'am, I am not a Pinkerton man. I'm just a detective who has been hired by the Contiello family to find their son. Please call me Quincy. I'm here to ask a few questions about the evening that Mr. Contiello went missing. Did you see anything?"

"Then you must call us Mabel and Henry if we're going to be on first name basis. Yes, we did see some of what happened. We already told the sheriff but we could tell you if you want to listen to it again," Mabel said.

"Please do." He sipped the coffee. Too thin. Nothing like what he'd had at the Black Swan earlier. He picked up a cookie and bit into it. A bitter burst of baking soda almost choked him. It took every bit of concentration to keep tears from his eyes.

"Well, it's like this. Henry was sitting on the porch. We didn't even go out there for a week after Ella died. The flu you know. We figured it was past, it'd been weeks since anyone had it in Huttig, but oh, no, Ella has to take it and we have to stay in the house for fear it would jump across the pine trees between us and her and we'd get it. Even though those girls couldn't open the hotel for three weeks, we figured we could still go out on the porch after supper, you know. I don't know how they'll run that hotel. I'm not even sure it's proper. Three young girls like that with men in the rooms upstairs. It just don't look right. I don't sup-pose Bridget is plannin' on goin' back to El

51

Dorado even though she has a home there. She always was a handful. Pretty as a picture and the boys flocked around her like flies on garbage. Not that I'm sayin' she is trash but that's the way boys were. From the time she took her hair out of pig tails they were sittin' on the porch wantin' to get a smile from her. She's flighty. She ain't goin' to be a bit of help to Catherine. I expect she could run a hotel but them other two ain't nothing but a hindrance to her. Alice has feathers for brains and Bridget thinks because she's pretty she doesn't have to work." Mabel finally picked up her cup and sipped the coffee.

Quincy had the urge to shake his head to remove all the unnecessary information.

"Now, darlin', you know Quincy, here didn't come over to hear you talk about what goes on next door all the time. He wants to know about that night when Ralph went missing. Let me tell it. I was sittin' on the side porch. I went out the kitchen door since we'd just had our supper. I think Mabel made us fried pork chops that night. She makes almighty good pork chops. You know what most people do wrong, they cook them too long. Anyway, it wasn't quite dark yet and I heard an automobile drive up at the hotel. I started on over there to

52

tell whoever it was not to waste their time since the doctor said they couldn't open back up for three weeks. I made it to the edge of the yard. You know from the side porch you can't see the hotel too good with all the pine trees so I had to walk up to the edge of the front yard. When the company built houses they had quite a job of clearing land to put the houses in amongst the trees in so they didn't take out more trees than they had to. Did you know that Huttig isn't a very old town? It was built so that the saw mill workers would have a place to bring their families and all. We come here in 1903 with the first of the bunch. I'd been working over at the mill a couple of years by then and me and Mabel got one of the first company houses. We been here ever since. Brought four sons with us but they're all grown and got families of their own now. Work over at the mill just like I did. I still go in two days a week and help out," he said.

"Henry, tell the man what you saw," Mabel said.

"Oh, that. Well, I could see it was Ralph all right and the way he slammed that door he wasn't right happy. Couldn't say I would be either if my wife went against what I told her. Not that I'd ever raise a hand to a woman, but that Bridget, she was a handful. He stormed into the hotel and then I heard a mess of screamin' and a pop like someone slamming a door and everything went quiet. I turned my good ear that way to see if I could hear him bein' mean to her but I didn't so I just mosied on back into the house."

"Did you hear him leave?"

"Nope, didn't hear that. Me and Mabel got to cracking some of last year's pecans in at the kitchen table. I got a brother over in Oklahoma and he's got the biggest old pecan trees in his pasture. Must have fifty trees. When he come to visit he brought a hundred pounds and we been cracking them so Mabel can use them in her cookies. She didn't put any in these, though. Why didn't you Mabel?"

"I made them with and without. Some folks don't like the flavor so I just left the ones with pecans in the kitchen. Would you rather have that kind?" She asked Quincy.

"No ma'am, these are just fine," he said. "I appreciate your help and the refreshments but I must go. There are several other people I'd like to talk to this morning."

"Then go see Lizzy Brody over on the other side of the Swan. She don't have so many trees between her and the hotel and she told me she saw him leaving that night. We talked all about it after the sheriff come down here. I bet poor Ralph's momma is just sick with worry. That man ought to have a care and at least get in touch with his folks. If my boys treated me like that I'd jerk their ears right off the sides of their heads, even if they are past thirty years old." Mabel talked all the way to the front door.

Quincy settled his hat and tipped the brim. "Again, my thanks."

"Any time. You come on back over here if you want to talk about it again. We'll think hard and see if we remember anything else. Tell the O'Shea girls we would've brought over some food when Ella passed, God rest her soul, she was a good woman, that Ella was, but we was afraid we'd get the flu," Mabel said.

"I will do that," he said.

He knocked on Lizzy Brody's door and was surprised to see a young woman with a baby on her hip open it. "Hello, you must be that Pinkerton man who's lookin' into Ralph Contiello's disappearance. Come on in. I'm ironing so you'll have to talk while I work. With five kids, a body hasn't got time to sit and gab all day."

He followed her into the kitchen. She put the baby on a pallet and set a flat iron on the stove to heat, removed the hot one and went to work on a pillow case.

"You can sit if you'd like. I don't know a lot. I was out in the yard hauling my oldest boy, Clark, into the house when I saw Ralph come out of the hotel, get in the car and drive away. That's it. I told the sheriff."

"What time was this?" Quincy asked.

"Barely dark. After supper. Clark wanted to play out in the yard for a little while after we ate. I went out to bring him inside. It was a pretty day but the night air was a little nippy."

"Did you actually see Ralph get in the car? Was he mad?"

"Hey, I didn't go over there and ask the man if he was mad. Not me. Bridget says he's got a temper and he was leaving without her so I figured he wouldn't be wanting to talk to me. Besides I didn't know him well enough to even say 'hello,' much less go visiting about his wife and problems. He walked out the front door, got in his car and left."

"You sure it was Ralph?"

"I'd know that hat and fancy suit anywhere. Ain't no sawmill worker able to buy such fancy things. Besides, who else would have the keys to his car?"

"Why did Bridget marry such a man?

56

Mabel says the boys surrounded her like bees around honey," Quincy pried.

"Reckon it was to get away from a saw mill town. You'll have to ask her, though. It didn't work, did it? She's right back where she started. Anything else?"

"No, that would be all. Thank you." Quincy said.

"Let yourself out the door if you don't mind."

He did and went back to the hotel, picked up his kit and went to work on the O'Sheas' automobile. Not that he expected to find a thing in it. If Ralph Contiello was killed in that house, they wouldn't be so stupid as to load him up and haul him away. If he died there, he was buried there.

Quincy groaned. He hated to use a shovel.

It was a lovely spring morning so Catherine took her book to the front porch. Lunch was ready to serve but there wouldn't be many willing to venture out to the Swan on the first day. They'd leave it to the foolish to see if there were flu germs still lingering about behind the cabbage rose wallpaper in the lobby. Or maybe they hid under the beds upstairs and would creep down to leap upon unsuspecting guests while they were eating pot roast and pound cake. A person just never knew about flu germs. They were devious creatures.

Catherine kept her head tilted downward as if reading, but her eyes kept straying above the words to the man in the front yard with his tools going over every square inch of their Model T. He had a little brush and some kind of powdery looking substance, a magnifying glass and a note book.

He could rake and scrap until hell froze over but he wouldn't find a thing. She'd been extra careful and then cleaned the Ford twice with lye soap. He wouldn't find a single thing that belonged to Ralph. She'd known in the beginning that the Contiello's would send someone fancy to find their son and she'd done what she could.

Good luck. You won't find squat Mr. Fancy Man. Just get finished and go on back to the rich people who raise sons to disrespect their women and tell them that you couldn't find a thing to suggest foul play. Because you won't, Mr. Pinky. I was very, very careful.

Neither Catherine, Alice nor Bridget had told a lie, not to the sheriff or to Quincy. They had simply not told the whole truth. Catherine replayed the night after Ella's funeral in her mind. They'd known he would come after Bridget and they had already decided she was not going back with him, not ever. She'd taken her last beating. The week before Catherine had talked to a lawyer and he'd said it wouldn't be easy but he would help Bridget get a divorce.

Ralph had barreled through the front door like a bear with a sore tooth. He didn't even stop in the lobby but took the steps two at a time, screaming for Bridget the whole time, telling her what he intended to do to her for not listening to him.

Catherine intended to step between them but she barely made it across the lobby when she heard the pop and Ralph tumbled, hind end over tea kettle, to the bottom of the stairs. His eyes were wide open and he wasn't breathing. If he had been, Catherine would have seen to it he stopped before he regained consciousness. Blood oozed out a head wound and soaked into the braided rug. She'd hated to lose that nice rug since her mother had made it just before she died, but the sacrifice was well worth it.

Bridget had gone into shock and threw the gun. It bounced off Ralph's chest and landed between him and the front door. Alice marched down the stairs, stepped over his body and said she was making tea.

"He's dead and I'm glad," she'd said.

Catherine's mind had gone a thousand different ways. What to do with him so the

Contiello family wouldn't put Bridget in jail was the first and foremost thing. It was only a few minutes before she helped Bridget to the kitchen but it seemed like eternity.

"You didn't kill him. Good Lord, girl, that bullet barely grazed his head," she'd told Bridget a dozen times before she'd managed to calm her.

"But there's blood," she'd argued.

"Yes, the bullet nicked the side of his head but that wouldn't kill him. It might soften up his hard head but it dang sure didn't kill the sorry excuse of a man. It was the fall that broke his neck."

"What'll we do about this?" Alice had asked. "We can't leave him layin' there. He'll stink by tomorrow."

"We're going to get rid of the body," Catherine had said.

"They'll come lookin' for him," Bridget had wailed.

"Of course they will and we'll tell them the truth. He came and you threatened him with a gun, even shot at him but the bullet missed and stuck in the wall. We must have scared him because he left," Catherine had told her.

That's exactly what they'd done, and the story got easier with each telling.

■ ■ ■ ■

Quincy finally shut all the doors and carried his kit to the porch. He set it down and leaned against a porch post, rolling his shirt sleeves down and buttoning them at the cuffs.

Catherine wished he'd leave them rolled up so she could see all that dark soft hair on his arms. She wondered if he had a mat like that on his chest and then blushed at her own thoughts.

"Find anything?"

"Nothing. It's almost too clean," he answered.

"Of course it is. We took Momma to the doctor in it after she took sick so I scrubbed it clean twice. Once after we figured out she had the flu and once after she died so there wouldn't be a chance one of us girls would get it. The doctor suggested we scrub anything Momma was around," she said.

"Well, damn it all. You could have told me that before I spent two hours going over every square inch with a magnifying glass," he said.

"My, my, you have a temper Mr. Massey. You didn't ask me if we'd cleaned the car. If you had, I would have told you. Are you going to beat me for not telling you?" Catherine deliberately tormented him.

"I do not strike women," he said icily.

His jaw quivered in anger and he tried to firm his mouth into a hard line but it didn't work. They still looked soft and kissable. She wondered what it would be like to kiss those lips and felt another rush of scarlet heading from her neck to her face.

"I'm glad to hear that. Now what's your next order of business?" She asked.

"Lunch and then I'm going down to check Ralph's car. Maybe I'll find something in it to give me an idea of what happened," he said.

"You just might do that. No telling what you could find in there. After Bridget married into the family I found out all kinds of unsavory things about them. Of course, I never told Momma or anyone else. He never was faithful to her so you'll find other women's fingerprints, no doubt."

"I know about the Contiello family. I know about Ralph and his indiscretions. I also know that he was abusive. What I want to know is where he is," Quincy said.

"Then find out," Catherine said.

"Oh, honey, I intend to find out and if you are at the bottom of the pile when I get through sorting through all this information, I will have the sheriff arrest you."

"I'll be sittin' right here at the Black Swan. You find evidence that I killed that man and you can put the hand cuffs on me yourself." She held out her wrists.

"Don't tease me, Miss O'Shea."

"Don't threaten me, Pinky."

CHAPTER FOUR

Dark clouds covered the sun just before supper time on Thursday. It had been a nice spring day, a bit nippy in the morning but the sun warmed it by early afternoon. It was beginning to look like rain which could either slow Quincy down or make his job miserable. Either way if the clouds produced what they threatened, southern Arkansas was about to get into its rainy season.

Quincy didn't like the tall pine area of the state as well as he liked the rolling hills around Little Rock. He sure wasn't going to like turning over the entire garden, which looked to be about twelve by thirty feet. Plenty big enough to hide a body, or two or three.

He'd been in town almost a week and hadn't found a single thing to link the ladies of the Black Swan to Ralph's car. He'd matched Bridget's fingerprints on the passenger side of the car, and like Catherine had said, there were multiple unidentifiable prints in the back seat. The steering wheel netted a couple that could have belonged to Ralph but certainly didn't match the ones he'd taken from the ladies.

More than anything, he'd like go back to Little Rock. If he were completely honest with himself, he wanted to run from the crazy feelings he had every time he was near Catherine. Granted she was a lovely lady with all that deep red hair, creamy skin, and dark green eyes that could see straight into his soul. But Quincy didn't have time for such things in his world. Perhaps admitting failure and going back to Little Rock wouldn't be such a bad idea if he could get away from the Black Swan.

He was sitting in a small café across from the mill hoping to find someone who might remember something about Ralph when an old man pulled out a chair at his table and sat, uninvited. "Reckon you'd be that fancy Pinkerton man that's got the whole town in a stir. If'n I was you I'd get on with myself and hurry out of town. There's a dozen women already plannin' ways to drag your sorry hind end to the altar."

Quincy's eyes widening had nothing to do with the strong coffee he'd been sipping.

"Reckon I'd get that scared look too if I

was your age. I also reckon that you're fair game by now. The O'Shea girls haven't let it out they're interested. Catherine ain't wantin' you. Alice don't know what she wants and Bridget is still married, legally. So the other women will circle like a pack of hungry coyotes and the strongest one will win. There ain't nothin' here about old Ralph and you done covered the whole town and everyone has told you what they know. So get on the last train and go on back to wherever you come from. You know why Ralph married Bridget? Because she was a good girl from a little bitty place. She didn't know what he was and she give him a pretty front for his dirty business. I expect one of those people that he or his family cheated or a family member of someone they had killed showed up and fed him to the gaters down across the border. That's the way I see it."

"And who are you?" Quincy asked.

"I'm Major Engram. That's not a title. It's a name. Momma thought it sounded good. I been a saw mill man my whole life. Live a couple of houses down that way." He pointed toward the right. "Lost my wife two years ago and two daughters to the flu last fall. My sons-in-law are saw mill men. They remarried and the new wives are good to me but they ain't blood. Got grandkids that are and I take comfort in them."

"I'm glad to meet you Mr. Engram. Where were you that night Ralph went missing?"

"Where I always am. Went home. Eat my supper. Sat on the porch since it was a fair night. Only thing I saw was Alice out walking but that ain't so unusual. She's out walking ever so often or ridin' that bicycle of hers. Pretty girl ain't she? Too bad she's a little light in the upstairs department."

So Alice had been out that night. She hadn't mentioned it when she told the story. That just might be the chink in their armor. He couldn't wait to get back to the Swan and ask them about that little forgotten item.

"So you going to outrun these women with wedding rings on their minds?" Major asked.

"Maybe when my work is finished. I think I can run faster than any of them," Quincy teased.

"Then you ain't got a lick of common sense, feller. Once a woman sets her mind, you can't run far enough or fast enough. You will be caught and there's a whole town full has set their heads. One of them will have you. Too bad it ain't Catherine. She's got the most sense of any woman left in

Huttig. Got it from her Momma. That Ella was a good woman. Alice is more like Patrick. Always chasin' a butterfly."

"Thank you for the visit," Quincy said. "You reckon you can keep them at bay if they come in here lookin' for me?"

"I'll do my best son, but I'm sixty years old. They'll run rough shod over me pretty quick. You'd best just look both ways and run like hell."

"Come by the Black Swan some evening and I'll buy you supper," Quincy offered as he straightened his tie and settled his hat.

"I'll come on Tuesday. I like Catherine's pot roast. It's too damn bad about what happened to Ira. She has what it woulda took to make him a good man."

Quincy nodded. So there was another story, about some man named Ira, hiding in the woodwork, too. Had he gone missing, also?

He found all three sisters in the kitchen. Bridget looked more than a little pale and was sipping hot tea. Lord, he hoped she wasn't coming down with the flu, and he caught it. Alice hummed as she took a pan of hot yeast rolls from the oven. Catherine was slicing apple pies into six sections. After only two days the restaurant business was back in full swing.

"Oh, Mr. Massey, you have company on the upper floor tonight. A salesman from Crossett has checked in for three days. His name is Jed," Alice said.

"Why didn't you tell me you'd been out walking around town on the night Ralph disappeared?" He asked bluntly.

"Because you didn't ask," she said.

"Did you see anyone or anything unusual?"

"No. I sketched the moon that night. I sat on a stump between here and the Commercial. We'd just buried Momma and I wanted to capture the night on paper so I could remember her. You want to see it?" Alice asked.

"Another time. Is it safe for a woman to be out after dark alone?"

"Really, Mr. Massey, this is Huttig, not El Dorado or Little Rock. Everyone knows everyone here. Besides . . ." She lowered her voice to a whisper. ". . . they all think I'm a little touched you know. Superstition has it that if you hurt a person who's dim witted, you'll have bad luck."

Whoa! Alice isn't as simple minded as folks think. He'd put that in his notes and see where it might lead.

"Anything else?" Bridget asked.

"No, I suppose not," Quincy said. "Supper smells good. Don't suppose I could have a piece of that pie to hold me over?"

Catherine put a slice on a plate and handed it to him. "Of course. You can have anything you want. We'll just add it to your bill."

Their fingers touched again and the feelings it evoked sent them both into an emotional upheaval. Quincy looked up from the pie and into her eyes. Without a doubt she felt it, too. Her eyes had gone from brittle to soft and he liked the transformation.

Catherine saw past his dark eyes and into his soul. He was a lonely man who wanted affection but had no idea how to go about obtaining it.

It felt like the room stood still for an hour. Actually, it was less than two seconds from the time their fingertips brushed and he hurriedly took his pie to the dining room.

"Now just what was that?" Alice asked.

"What was what?" Catherine slipped her hand into her apron pocket.

"He looked at you like he wanted to trade that chunk of pie for a kiss," Alice said.

Bridget shook her head. "You are always wandering around with your head up in the air. Catherine has better sense than to get mixed up with a man like that. She doesn't even know him. He might be another Ralph."

"Thank you," Catherine said.

But Quincy wasn't another Ralph. He was sure enough of himself that he didn't need to whip a woman to feed his ego. Not that she was about to argue with either Bridget or Alice. She couldn't even sort through her feelings much less present an intelligent explanation to either of them for the way her heart skipped beats when Quincy touched her.

That evening, when Catherine and Bridget settled into rocking chairs on the front porch, Catherine's mind traveled back again to that night.

Ralph was dead, ruining her mother's rug with his blood. Bridget was hysterical. She just hoped Alice could do the job she'd sent her to do without botching it up but she hadn't had a choice. There was just the three of them and they had to do the best they could. Alice could wear Ralph's clothing. Bridget was too emotional. Catherine was too tall.

Catherine and Alice had stripped Ralph of his trousers, shirt, vest, jacket, leaving him in his union suit and socks. Alice didn't even flinch at the blood on his collar as she dressed in his clothing. She was the one who suggested stuffing the toes of his shoes with newspapers so they wouldn't flop on her heels. She'd packed her own dress and jacket in the small case she carried around town when she sketched and without a backward glance stuffed her hair up under his hat and walked out the front door, as cool as a glass of lemonade on a hot sultry summer afternoon.

An hour later she returned dressed in her normal clothing and a sketch of the moon and pine trees in her kit along with Ralph's clothing. She unpacked his clothing from the case and they'd redressed him before they rolled him up in an old bedspread. Alice sewed the edges shut and suggested they wait until after midnight when the whole town would be sleeping to take him out of the house.

Even Catherine was surprised. Alice had a reputation for not having it altogether and she'd been the calmest one of the bunch. She'd reassured Bridget that getting rid of his body was the only way to keep her out of jail and alive. She'd done a major portion of the dirty work and to this day, she maintained that Ralph was evil and God had turned his eyes elsewhere when the man died.

■ ■ ■ ■

Catherine jumped when their new guest, Jed, made a racket when he opened the door to the porch. He sat down in a chair and began to rock. "Nice evening. Good little breeze."

"Yes, it is pleasant this evening," Bridget said.

"And you are Alice?" He asked.

"I'm Bridget. This is Catherine. Alice is off sketching something to paint."

"And I'm Jed Tanner, in case you've forgotten my name. I expect it's hard to keep up with names when you have so many coming and going all the time. Where's the detective?"

"Off detecting," Bridget said.

"He find out anything about that man that disappeared, yet?"

Catherine's nerves went as tight as a freshly laced turkey ready for the oven. "You've only been here a few hours. How'd you hear about it?"

"In the dining room during supper. Would you like to talk a walk and show me what Huttig looks like in the evening?" He deftly changed the subject. If he could get one of them alone he could pry information a lot quicker and better.

"No, I've put in a long day. Maybe another time." Catherine could smell a rat and the odor wasn't pleasant.

Had Jed really been interested in saw mill business he would have been staying at the Commercial. Unless it was booked solid, and she doubted that at this time of year. So exactly what was he doing in Huttig and why was he asking questions about Quincy?

"Back so soon?" Bridget looked up as Quincy opened the gate and headed toward the porch. The night clerk had called to tell him that the man who'd stayed in the room next to Ralph's had checked in again, if Quincy wanted to question him.

"The man had no more information. Said he didn't see anything. Heard the door in the next room open and someone prowling around, after a few minutes he heard it open and close a second time and someone walking on the balcony. I guess the only thing left is to start digging. You got a problem with that?" He looked at Catherine.

"Just put all the dirt back where you find it," she said.

"What on earth are you digging for? Do you think Ralph is dead and hiding here on this place?" Jed asked.

"It'll convict or clear. One way or the

other we'll know." Quincy didn't take his eyes from Catherine. Just one time he wished she'd act flustered when he talked about digging up her property.

"I'm going inside. It's getting chilly out here," Bridget said.

"Me, too. I must compliment you ladies on your fine cooking. I'd heard the Black Swan was as good a restaurant as hotel and the report was surely true," Jed said.

Catherine sat still, but she did murmur a thank you as Jed and Bridget disappeared inside the house. She listened intently for a moment then heard his footsteps on the stairs and the door shut into their private quarters. At least he hadn't gotten Bridget alone to question her. Catherine would have to warn her sisters about Jed. If he was a bona fide salesman she'd . . . what . . . she wondered how she'd punish herself if she was wrong about the man. Why, she'd kiss Quincy, that's what she'd do. She was glad the sun had set because she blushed so crimson her face felt like it had been leaning into an open fire.

Quincy melted his long body into a white rocking chair, removed his hat and feathered back his dark hair with a sweep of his hand. "So tell me how Ira went missing."

She bristled. "That is none of your business."

"Did he ever turn up or am I going to find more than one body in your garden plot?"

"You are an insensitive cad. Good night, Mr. Massey." She stood up and marched ramrod straight into the house.

He'd finally broken through her thick skin and was about to congratulate himself when Alice appeared from the back side of the house. She carried a small kit, not unlike a suitcase in her right hand. She was dressed in those abominable overalls and two long ropey braids hung down her back.

"Good evening," she said brightly.

"You been out sketching the moon again?" Quincy asked coolly.

"No, tonight I was working on a pine tree with a big hoot owl sitting on a lower branch. I saw him there a week ago and have been checking at different times hoping to see him again. I was so excited to see him there tonight. Where are Catherine and Bridget? Inside?"

"Tell me about Ira," Quincy hoped the abrupt change of subject would catch her off guard.

She set her kit on the porch and pulled up a chair. "What do you want to know?"

"Who is he? When did he disappear? Did

he know Ralph? Is there a chance they disappeared together? Anything you know."

"Those are pretty stupid questions," she said.

"Will you answer them anyway?"

"I suppose I will. You're going to feel dumb, though. Ira McNewell was the kindest man in Huttig. He was quiet and sweet and engaged to Catherine. Then the war came. She didn't want him to go. He didn't have to because he had a limp from a saw mill accident. Tree fell the wrong way and broke his leg. It didn't heal right and it caused the limp. But Ira felt strong about our country and he was very determined. They fought about it but he won and she figured they wouldn't take him anyway but she was wrong. He was good with machinery and they sent him overseas right away," Alice said.

That much made Quincy squirm.

She continued. "Anyway the flu hit this whole area hard and both of Ira's parents went with it. Catherine sent him a letter and it came back. Then his sister and brother died and their children. The whole McNewell family in Huttig was gone except for Ira. Catherine wrote him again and it came back. Then one day a telegram came for his parents and the man down at the

Company store brought it to Catherine because he didn't know what else to do with it. A year ago, Ira was killed in the war. They never found his body to bring it home to be buried with the rest of his family."

Quincy felt lower than a snake's belly and as insensitive as a house slug.

"I don't reckon he did know Ralph since by the time Ralph was coming around to court Bridget Ira was already off to the war so no, I'd have to say they didn't disappear together. Anything else?"

"One more thing. Would you ask Catherine if she would please join me on the porch for a moment?"

"I can do that. Are you really going to dig up our garden? Why?"

"Alice, if the O'Shea sisters are not guilty of anything, then I want to make sure they don't have a black cloud hanging over their lives. I'm going to find out what happened to Ralph because it's my job to do so."

"I see. Well, I'll send Catherine out. Goodnight."

"And a good-night to you," Quincy said.

Five minutes passed. Then ten. Finally the door opened after fifteen minutes. Catherine folded her hands over her chest and waited.

"I was terribly insensitive and rude. I owe you an apology. I am terribly sorry," he said.

"Is that all?"

"Yes, ma'am it is."

"Will you leave us alone then?"

"Not until I exhaust every possibility where Ralph is concerned. The way I see it is that it would have been very easy for Alice to dress in his clothing, drive to the Commercial in his car, wearing his hat and his gloves which would have kept any prints off the car, redressed in his room into her own clothing and simply walked back to the Swan. From the description I have of the man and the photograph, he wasn't very tall or heavy. If I figured that much out, then other people will also. Like I told Alice, I'll either find evidence to convict you or clear your names."

"The shovels are in the tool shed. There are three of them. Take your pick. Put whatever you use back clean when you're finished," Catherine said.

CHAPTER FIVE

A slow drizzle fell from a gray sky, leaving dew kisses on the pine needles and turning the garden area into a soupy mess. There was no way Quincy could dig in such sludge so he busied himself organizing all his notes to present to his father who was also his boss in Little Rock. Surely by the end of next week he'd head back north; failure for the first time, or case closed for so many times he'd stopped counting.

He had everything arranged in a notebook from the day the sheriff had brought him to the Black Swan until that very evening. Now all he had to do was type them up on the Underwood typewriter he carried with him. He'd just laid his pen aside when his stomach set up a growl. It was lunch time and Friday was home made soup, cornbread and blackberry cobbler day. He shut the door to his room at the same time Jed stepped out into the hallway.

"Do you really think you'll find that body in the garden or under the rose bushes? Or do you think someone took him far away from this little burg?" Jed asked.

"I thought you had business with the saw mill today?"

"Oh, that, well, it got postponed until tomorrow." Jed waved his hands in a gesture of dismissal and followed Quincy to the dining room.

The room was filled but at least there weren't people waiting in the lobby for a seat. Conversation kept a steady hum in the room. All three O'Shea sisters breezed in and out of the kitchen with trays, serving patrons and taking orders.

Jed spotted one table recently vacated near the kitchen door. Bridget had just finished wiping away cornbread crumbs and laying out fresh napkins and silverware.

"Shall we?" Jed motioned toward the table.

Quincy nodded and they made their way through the crowd of strangers to the corner. Catherine brought two coffee cups, filled them, and promised to return with the rest of their lunch.

"So what is it that you sell?" Quincy asked.

"I sell words," Jed whispered.

"You're a writer? You told the O'Sheas you

were a salesman?"

"That I am. I didn't lie about being a salesman. I did tell a little white one about selling something to the mill. I couldn't take a chance of them throwing me out of the hotel. The story is right here and I can get to it easier if I'm in the middle rather than on the sidelines. I sell words to the highest bidder and I've got two big newspapers chomping at the bit for my story. I'm searching for the same thing you are. What happened to Ralph Contiello, the man whose father has ties with the biggest, most lucrative mafia boss in New York City? I'm here to see why a full blooded Sicilian allowed his son to marry a back woods Irish girl. I want an inside scoop on the story if she killed him. With all these women's rights there might even be more than one story," Jed said.

"I see."

"I'll pay for information."

"It's not for sale," Quincy said. He already knew it wasn't a little matter of a man disappearing in a saw mill town down near the Louisiana border. But if the press was already aware of all the connections and possible story lines, then God help Bridget and the whole O'Shea family if he did find a body hiding on their property.

"Here it is. Signal when you are ready for dessert." Catherine placed steaming bowls of soup in front of them and a platter of cornbread in the middle of the table. She deliberately let her hand brush against Quincy's. It was there: that oozy, warm sensation. She wanted to slap something, preferably Quincy's face. He had no right to come to Huttig and upset her world. They'd expected the Contiellos to go a step further than the county sheriff, but why, oh why, did they have to send a man that set her blood boiling with anger one minute and pure desire the next?

"Will you give me your word you won't rat me out?" Jed asked.

"I think it would be better if you went to the Commercial or one of the other small hotels. It'll be a mess when the O'Sheas find out. Maybe they'd cut you a little slack if you told the truth, but I doubt it," Quincy said.

"You think they'd tell me anything if I told them what I was after?"

"It's your skin." Quincy lifted a spoonful of soup to his mouth and made appreciative noises. It was chunked full of bite sized pieces of tender beef, had a thick red base with lots of potatoes, carrots, green beans and peas. There was a hint of something else, something a little warm on the tongue. Peppers, that was it. Mexican peppers he bet they grew in their garden.

"Do you think they did it?" Jed asked.

"I'm not paid to think. I'm paid to find evidence and report back to my boss."

Alice stopped to top off their coffee cups. "Think about what?"

"About Ralph and why he's missing and where he is," Quincy answered honestly. "I was just telling Mr. Tanner that I'm here to find evidence to support any theory that he was killed in this town or to disprove such a thing."

"I see." She was off to the next table.

"I think Mr. Massey is trying to prove us innocent rather than guilty," Alice told her sisters when she refilled her china coffee pot from the kitchen. "I heard him talking to Mr. Tanner and he was asking if we did it."

"I knew that man wasn't a salesman. He's probably another rotten detective," Catherine said.

"I've got a notion to go out there and admit what happened right in front of everyone in the dining room. I'm tired of this," Bridget said.

"*No, you will not!* We took care of it and we made a pact to never tell anyone," Catherine said. "Besides if you tell, they'll put us all in jail."

The steady drizzle kept everyone indoors that evening. Catherine read. Bridget knitted what appeared to be a pink baby shawl. Alice smeared paint on a canvas set up close to the business counter. All three would have rather been in their own quarters away from the two guests but they'd decided after much discussion to sit in the lobby until bedtime. Hopefully, it would convince both men that they weren't hiding anything.

Quincy held a newspaper in front of his face but keeping his mind on the articles was a chore. He kept peeking around the side at Catherine and then getting angry at himself for doing so. She was an Irish inn owner who wasn't over a war hero she'd been in love with before he died. Quincy had been to the war front but not in the capacity of a soldier; more of a spy and only for a short time. Another case closed and never mentioned. He could never compete with someone who'd laid down his life and died for the cause like Ira had done.

Catherine's mind wandered as her eyes went from word to word, page to page, not comprehending a single thing. Finally she laid the book on her lap and stared at Jed.

She'd always approached a problem head on, not unlike two bull calves in the springtime. Problem on one side; Catherine on the other. She usually won.

"So Mr. Tanner, what is it that you sell? Have you made progress with the mill boss?" She asked.

"Not yet. I'm hoping to see him tomorrow morning." Jed laid his cigar aside and went to watch the rain through the window.

"Mr. Tanner, I think you are lying to us," Alice said. "I do believe you are here for the same reason Mr. Massey is. He's told us the truth from the beginning but you are sneaking around, aren't you?"

A wide grin split Quincy's face but he kept it behind the newspaper. Alice might be considered slow witted but in all honesty she was outspoken and didn't give a damn about the proper rules of society.

"But . . ." Jed stammered.

Alice laid her brush down and cocked her head to one side. "I think you are trying to get one of us to talk about Ralph. Are you a detective?"

"No, I am not," Jed denied emphatically.

"Then who are you?" Catherine asked.

"I'm a freelance writer. I'm going to write a story about Ralph's disappearance. I would like your cooperation. I can give it a positive slant that you had no alternative but to kill him since he was abusing you, Bridget. With my ability and your confession we can go a long way for women's rights," he said.

"Your ability had better go up to your room, pack your bags and go on to the Commercial or one of the other hotels in town. We have no confessions to make. Slant your story however you want but you are not getting anything from us. I'll expect you back down here to settle your bill in ten minutes," Catherine said.

"But . . ." he stammered.

"No buts. Just go," Catherine said.

His eyes flashed and his fists clenched at his sides. "I'll paint you as the blackest hearted women in the South. I'll tell everyone that you . . ."

"I'd be careful if I were you. You could be treading on very dangerous ground," Quincy said.

Jed stopped half way up the stairs and looked back over his shoulder. "You're the one who should be careful. Be sure you're not giving up too soon just because you can't believe a woman could kill her husband."

"Have it your way." Quincy went back to his paper. Apparently the man had rotten eggs for brains. The Contiello family would not appreciate their name smeared in newspaper article, and Catherine could make the whole mafia look like school children if she went on the warpath.

"I'm going to my room," Bridget said.

"And I'm going to clean my brushes and go sketch a while in our quarters. I suppose you can take care of Mr. Tanner's final bill without us, Catherine?" Alice raised an eyebrow.

"I can take care of more than his final bill," Catherine said.

His suitcases bumped the walls and he practically fell on the new braided rug at the end of the steps. Catherine held her breath but the rug only shifted a few inches. It didn't skitter all the way out into the floor and leave the dark, irregular shaped stain they'd been unable to remove.

He paid his bill and left in a huff.

Catherine sat back down with her book and flipped back ten pages to begin again. Tomorrow the news would be all over town that she'd tossed out a paying customer on his ear, and in the rain, to boot. No doubt, Mr. Tanner would be out shaking every pine tree in Huttig, hunting for ugly things to say in his story about the Black Swan and its owners. At that moment, Catherine had more important things to think about, like how to control the urge to brush an errant strand of hair away from Quincy's broad forehead.

Quincy laid his paper in his lap. "You think that was a wise decision? You could have let him stay and then you could have kept an eye on him."

"I don't need to keep an eye on a cockroach. I just kill it so it doesn't produce more of its kind," she said.

"Sassy, ain't you?" He said.

"I prefer to think of it as honesty," she smarted back at him.

"Are you honest about everything? He asked.

"I've told you the truth."

"Can I ask you something personal?"

"Is it about Ralph?"

"No, it's about Bridget. Why did she stay with him?"

"Because he would have killed her before he'd let her go. It would have been a bad mark on the Contiello name. His family is only one generation away from being Catholic. His mother is Methodist and was elated that Bridget shared their religion. Our ancestors were Catholic also. Momma was but she converted to Daddy's faith. Anyway, you have to understand that much.

Catholics do not recognize divorce. But then religion aside, society puts a black mark on anyone who has a divorce. I know of only one man in Union County who's got one granted in the past two years. A woman never has up to now. The Contiellos are a proud bunch and they're very wealthy. Bridget had one choice. Stay with him until he killed her. A few years ago there was a case in Massachusetts about a woman who took her husband to court for beating her. Remember?"

Quincy nodded.

Catherine continued. "The court said a man had the right to beat his wife with a reasonable instrument. That time it was a bull whip. I suppose Ralph figured a belt or his fists wasn't nearly so bad. He might even think he's a good husband for keeping her in line. But I'm glad he's gone and she'll get that divorce. It'll take a while but we will fight to the death for it. The Contiellos will try to block it but Daddy was close friends with the judge of Union County. I'm hoping that helps."

"Why divorce him if he's gone?" Quincy asked.

"Because she wants her maiden name back and that's going to be a touchy thing. I don't know of a woman in our part of the world who has ever gotten the court to allow such a thing," Catherine said.

"Again, why?"

"Last week Doctor Jones confirmed her suspicions. If you tell Jed this I'll have your head on a chopping block and a butcher knife in my hand, but she's expecting a baby. She doesn't want it to be a Contiello. She wants it to be an O'Shea. If the Contiellos know she's expecting their grandchild, they'll take it from her."

"But that would make the child illegitimate."

"Better to think its father is a mill worker or the town drunk than a Contiello. We don't really care at this point about opinions. We care about protecting Bridget. She made a big mistake with that smooth talkin' Italian. I wish he'd have never come to Huttig. If the Commerical hadn't been filled that night, he wouldn't have stayed here and things wouldn't have happened the way they did. Bridget was pretty and young and stupid. He was good looking, older and very wise."

"Was?" Quincy asked.

"As in yesterday. Is? Was? It's all a matter of speech. I'd rather you find him in my garden than have him come back and jerk Bridget back into his world."

"But she'd go to jail," Quincy said.

"And that would be better than living with him," Catherine said.

"I see. You have my promise that your secret is safe."

He meant it. He wouldn't even put it in his report, although it would go a long way in convincing a judge of their innocence. No woman would murder her child's father. Even a bad father was better than growing up illegitimate.

"Thank you. Are you really going to dig up our flowers and garden?" She asked.

"Yes, I am. Any place I can find that looks suspicious — like it's been turned over in the past month — I intend to check. You got something to tell me?"

"Not a thing. So tell me, Mr. Massey, where did you grow up? Little Rock?"

"No, ma'am. I'm from Oklahoma. Little place called Tonkawa," he said.

"Indian blood?" She asked.

"My father."

"That's strange. Never thought of an English name like Massey being Indian," she said.

"You have a quick mind. Massey is English, as was my mother."

"I've pried. Forgive me. It's none of my business," she blushed.

Quincy took a deep breath and began. "She and my father were very much in love. It was 1889, back before statehood. He was a teacher at an Indian school not far from where she lived. Her father was in government and sent to Oklahoma to take care of the land rush and that kind of thing. Anyway, they were going to elope but he was killed the week before. He was in the wrong place at the wrong time. Two men faced off in the street and the bullet killed him as he was coming out of the general store. I was born eight months later. She refused to marry the man my grandfather lined up to keep her reputation from going up in flames and never married anyone else. My grandfather disowned her and went back to Washington D.C. She stayed on as a teacher at the Indian school and raised me. She got the flu last fall and died," he said.

Catherine was in shock. Her arch rival and enemy had just told her a very intimate part of his history. She was tongue tied for the first time in her life.

"I'm so sorry," she said.

"Thank you. I expect you do know how I feel since you lost your father last fall and just recently, your mother. The epidemic was horrible. I went to college and then was recruited into the service as a spy. From there it wasn't difficult for a detective agency to put me on their payroll. Thanks for listening and I'd rather not have all that branded about, either," he said.

"Your story is as safe with me as mine is with you," she said.

She laid her book aside with intentions of heading for their private quarters but her foot had fallen asleep and she stumbled. Quincy caught her mid-air before she hit the floor.

"My foot," she mumbled.

Catherine wasn't a tiny wisp of a woman. She stood five foot seven inches so it took a big man to hold her in his arms and Quincy did without effort. The warmth of his arms caused giant butterflies in her stomach. She felt like a band of gypsies were whirling around inside her head, bright colors spiraling every which way like silk scarves in sunlight.

Before she could calm her heart which had set about thumping like a base drum in a parade, Quincy gently ran the palm of his hand down her cheek, barely touching it, soft as the wings of a Monarch butterfly fluttering across her raw nerve endings. Nothing Ira had ever done made her feel so vulnerable and she damn sure didn't like the feeling. But she couldn't pull away. Her body kept begging for one more moment in his arms.

He leaned down, his eyes half open.

She tiptoed and shut hers firmly. She would have this kiss and then she'd slap lightning bolts from his face. She was fully convinced that the moment his lips touched hers she would feel nothing but revulsion.

She was wrong.

When they broke away she wanted more.

"I'm sorry. That should not have happened," he said.

"Why?"

"Because I'm on the job and you . . ."

"Did you kiss me and tell me all those things about yourself in hopes that I'd feel all mushy and confess that I'd killed Ralph?" She asked.

"I did not," he protested.

"Then don't be sorry. I'm dang sure not. I don't expect this to lead to one thing, Mr. Massey. But as kisses go, it was all right. Good night," she said.

It was Quincy's turn for shock.

All right! That kiss made my knees go weak. It made my head spin. And you say it's just all right. God Almighty, you are more desirable than any woman I've ever known and it's just all right?

"Good night, Catherine," he muttered.

She forced her tingling foot and boneless legs to carry her to the door into the living room of their quarters. Throwing herself down on the sofa, she sighed. The kiss was more than all right but nothing could ever come of it, so why let him think she was all sweet on him? Better he think she was a loose woman who kissed many men in her past than know that he was only the second in a very short line. Ira had kissed her twice before he went to the war, once when he'd proposed and once when he left. Both had been dry brushes across her lips. Nothing that left her whole body begging for more. So that's what it was like to be really kissed.

"You're positively glowing," Alice said.

"It's a bit warm," Catherine told her.

"He kissed you, didn't he? He's been wanting to since the day the sheriff brought him here."

"My Lord, Alice, I'm still in mourning for Ira."

"Ira? Well, you never did love him. You would have married him but you didn't love the man. He didn't set your blood to boiling like Mr. Massey."

"I did love Ira," Catherine protested. "Why would I say I'd marry him if I didn't love him?"

"Who knows? Maybe you were afraid of

being an old maid. I don't know why you do the things you do anymore than you know why I'm different from everyone else. But you didn't love Ira and you'd better be careful or you're going to get your heart broke by that man."

"Don't worry. I'm not going to ever kiss him again and he's not going to break my heart. It's not up for grabs."

"Don't make promises you don't intend to keep," Alice smiled sweetly.

The glow was still there when Catherine went to bed.

CHAPTER SIX

The work shed at the back corner of the vegetable garden was little more than a lean-to. It had three sides, a slanted roof, and two large doors hinged with straps of leather that moaned when Quincy eased them open. Just as Catherine said, three shovels were lined up on the back wall close to a bicycle that looked as if it was used regularly. She'd said they'd worked together to turn over the dirt in the garden. He sincerely hoped it was in preparation to plant onion sets and potatoes and not a dead body.

He touched all three shovels. No visions of Ralph or the way he died appeared by touching the tools. Not a single jolt of desire shot through his body so he had no idea which one Catherine had used. They were simply tools for digging, which is something he really hated to do. He picked one and carried it along with a belly full of aggravation to the garden.

Catherine opened the back door of the hotel at the same time he turned over the first shovel of dirt. He wore bibbed overalls and a soft red flannel shirt and looked as much out of place as a duck in the Sahara desert. She almost felt sorry for him, but the feeling passed quickly. This was the reason she'd insisted they dig the garden; the reason why she'd been adamant about moving the lilac bush and repositioning the rose bushes. By the time he got through digging and finding nothing, he'd be tired of badgering them and go on down the road. And that would be a day for rejoicing. She'd dance a jig on the blood stain at the bottom of the stairs when Quincy left the Black Swan for good.

At least she thought she would until her heart tumbled to the pits of her soul and tears welled up behind her deep green eyes. Now what in the devil was all that about? She wanted him gone; this thing settled and in the past so why did she dread seeing him leave ten times worse than the day Ira left Huttig for the war?

"You're really going to let me dig aren't you?" His heavy black brows knit together into one line above his dark eyes.

"Yes, sir. It'll break up the clods and we can get our onions and potatoes in the ground when you are finished. If you'll stomp that shovel around when you turn over each bunch, it would be a great help," she said.

Holy Mary, he'd like to strangle her. She was trying to outwit him by telling him to go right ahead. A part of him was terrified he'd find the body right there. In the past few days he'd walked all over the small town and found only a couple of other gardens. Most women grew a few tomatoes or cucumbers in a barrel or in their flower beds. Their husbands put in hard, long days at the mill and didn't have the energy or the time to uproot fifty foot pine trees to make way for garden space. Not many would fight the pine needle problem if they did. Of the two gardens he did find, one had been tilled in the past week with a plow and mule. The other hadn't been turned over since spring of the previous year. If Ralph had died that night in the hotel and the O'Shea women had buried his body, it had to be in this garden or under a lilac bush.

"What am I going to find, Catherine?" He asked.

"Probably a bunch of grub worms. I'll bring out a jar. Put the worms in it, please and I'll go fishing this evening after supper. Seems like it's going to be a fine day. Catfish might be biting," she said.

He gritted his teeth. "How deep should I dig?"

"All the way to China if you've a mind to do so, but aren't most graves about six feet deep? I wouldn't go further than that. If you want to believe me, we only dug down a foot when we worked over the garden a couple of weeks ago, but if you want to go six feet, have at it," she said.

"Women!" He grumbled.

She brought a jar and placed it at the edge of the plot, tucked her arms into the bib of her overalls and watched him for a spell before going back to the porch and sitting on the bottom step. She should be in the kitchen but Alice already had the chocolate pies made; they'd baked the pound cakes on Monday afternoon; and the pot roasts were in the oven. Bridget had the tables set and ready for the first rush of customers. And it was just so danged fun to sit and watch him work at a job he hated: teach him to doubt her word. Besides, the jar was half full of worms and she hadn't been fishing since her father passed away.

"Want me to bring your lunch out here to the back porch or are you plannin' on clean-in' up?" she asked when she heard the first lunch customers parking their automobiles and wagons in the front yard.

"Who said I have to clean up? Isn't my money good whether I'm in a suit or overalls?" He was irritated and with good reason. First, he didn't want to find a body. Second, he did want to so this job would be finished. Third, he was confused as the devil and Catherine was the only one in front of him, so she could take the brunt for leading him on a wild goose chase.

"Wash your hands and face and come right in. I'll charge your account no matter what you wear." She dusted off the seat of her overalls and went inside.

That gesture annoyed him. Lord, he hated overalls. They seemed to ask a man to look at a woman's fanny.

Not all men are like you, his conscience chided. *Some of them will feel sorry for her because she's lost so much and won't be thinking about what she's wearing or the dust on her tail.*

"Yes, they will," he mumbled as he set the shovel beside the porch post and went inside. It took him ten minutes to wash the dirt from behind his ears, out of his eyebrows and hair and at least make himself halfway presentable.

He found an old friend waiting in the lobby when he reached the bottom of the stairs. Seated on the edge of a high backed chair, Major Engram looked as out of place as a chicken at a coyote convention. His hat in his hand, he smiled when Quincy entered the room.

"Hmmph, here I thought you was right up there next to the President of the U.S. of A. in your fancy pants suits and here you are lookin' like me. You said you'd buy me dinner so I'm here to collect," Major said.

"Be glad for your company. Are there any tables left?" Quincy nodded toward the dining room.

"I counted fifteen folks goin' that way since I been here and ain't no one come out yet. I reckon there's room for two old hard workin' fellers like us. You need a hand with all that diggin'?"

They walked into the room together and all conversation stopped.

"Guess they were talkin' about us?" Major whispered and chuckled.

A few guarded whispers followed them to the table against the north wall.

"So?" Major asked when they were seated.

"So what?"

"You need help diggin' up that garden? Heard you was doin' some real work around here. You got an extra shovel, I'll help," Major said.

"Would you be honest if you hit something or would you cover it up?" Quincy asked.

"Oh, I'd be honest. Only I couldn't swear I wouldn't slap it around with the blade a few times for what it done to Miss Bridget. Why, hello, Miss Catherine. I could smell that roast all the way in town. Had to have me some of it and Mr. Massey here is buyin' today," Major said.

"How are you Major? It's good to see you've escaped the flu." Catherine set a heaping plate of food in front of each of them.

"Oh, honey, I'm too old and tough for the flu to take me. I'm goin' to die of pure orneriness not the flu," he grinned.

"Been fishin' lately? They bitin'? Mr. Massey here has dug up a whole jar full of bait. I might go later after supper," she said.

"They was bitin' last night. Had catfish for my supper. Pretty late when I got home but I fried 'em up anyway," he said.

"Good, maybe I'll catch enough to put fish on the menu tomorrow. Enjoy your dinner."

After she left Major lit into the potatoes and carrots first. "Women know how to cook them so they ain't mushy and then pour that good thick dark gravy over them. This is the way a man was meant to eat."

"It is good," Quincy agreed. Almost too tired to lift his fork, he hoped Major was serious about his offer to help him.

"Guess you've outrun the women with marriage on their brain," Major said.

"Been working on it," Quincy said.

"Don't get lazy. They'll be back for another shot at the gold ring if Catherine decides to throw you back in the pond."

"What are you talking about?" Quincy asked.

"Them sparks that near set the place on fire, that's what I'm talkin' about. You two give off a flame when she's close by. Other women can see she's set her cap and they won't be botherin' you 'til she makes up her mind. It's the way of women folks. Besides ain't a woman in Huttig that'd tangle with Catherine. You think she got that red hair by being Irish? Huh-uh, son. The devil give it to her to let folks know she's got a temper."

Quincy shook his head. At least Major was entertaining. If he was working beside him that afternoon the time should pass quickly. The morning had dragged on like a slug across the kitchen floor. He couldn't get Catherine out of his mind with her sitting right there watching him like a hawk. Every time he sunk the shovel into the dark earth, he did it in fear he'd either hit something solid or chop into a face, hand or some other body part.

Quincy sopped gravy with a chunk of hot roll. "So how much you going to charge me to help make sure there're no dead bodies out there in the garden?"

"I just had dinner and it was mighty fine but I reckon I could eat some more of the same later on this evenin'. I'll help you dig for the price of my supper," Major said.

"That's all. You'll dig all afternoon for your supper?"

"You got it and some conversation. You go to the war?"

"Yes, but . . ."

"I don't care about the buts. Just tell this old man what it was like and what you saw," Major said.

"You got a deal," Quincy said. "You want chocolate pie or pound cake and peaches for dessert?"

"Both," Major said.

"Fair enough," Quincy motioned to Catherine and gave her their order.

"See I told you," Major said after she'd gone back to the kitchen.

"What?"

Major waved his hands in the air. "Sparks. Reckon that's why folks call it sparkin' a girl. I just never did see it so plain until today."

"You've got women on the brain," Quincy said.

"Maybe so but I seen what I seen. When she comes back you take close notice. You'll be surprised. Why, it's a wonderment how the hotel ain't goin' up in flames."

When Catherine brought their dessert Quincy could almost smell the imaginative smoke. He'd be glad to get finished and out of Huttig. Matter of fact, if he didn't get the digging done that day, he might be paying for five or six suppers the next night. If men were willing to work for food, he'd hire them for sure.

In the middle of the afternoon Catherine appeared on the back porch again. "Hey, you two, I forgot to tell you that the middle of the garden is where we plant our carrots and turnips and things that grow under the dirt. We dig it down about two feet so the ground will be soft enough for growth."

Quincy groaned.

Major chuckled. "Yes, ma'am. We'll be sure to break up the clods real good. I do like them carrots in my roast. Be a shame next winter if there wasn't any, now wouldn't it?"

"Think you'll have it done by supper?"

Catherine asked.

Major stopped and wiped sweat from his forehead. "I reckon we will. If you hadn't remembered the carrots we mighta got the flower beds done, too, but that might slow us down."

She brought them a cup of coffee and slice of chocolate pie in the middle of the afternoon. By dusk they finished the whole job and came in to supper. They sat at the same table and ate the same thing they'd had for lunch. Quincy looked tired enough to fall asleep in his food. Major's declared he would've gladly worked another day for good food.

"I'm finished digging. Thank God! The first train heading north after today, I'm going to be on it. I'm getting my things packed up and ready to get out of here," Quincy said.

"Oh, I thought you two was going fishin' tonight. I already figured on tagging along to keep it all proper," Major teased.

"I'm the one going fishing. Mr. Massey will be busy with other things now that he's proved I wasn't lying," Catherine said.

"Woman ain't got no business down on that river without a man around. Never know what kind of fools is down there of an evening," Major said seriously.

"You sound like my father. I'm mean enough to take care of myself." She playfully patted him on the shoulder.

"You going to let her go by herself?" Major asked Quincy.

"She's a grown woman. Don't think it would do any good for me to tell her to stay home. I think she does what ever she wants," Quincy said.

Somehow he felt as if he were being steam rolled into an evening with Catherine. Major wasn't as innocent as a lamb. Lord, he might have been the one who put an end to Ralph and was just yanking Quincy's chain.

"Well, times are a changin' for sure. Women's rights and all. Not that I cotton to beatin' a woman. Never laid a hand on my sweet wife in all the years we was married. But I don't think a woman oughta be down there on the river after dark by herself."

"I'll be fine. Could be I won't even go. I might cook those worms into a nice big pot of soup instead of going fishing," Catherine teased.

Major pretended to shiver. "I'd rather eat that soup than worry about you hurtin' some unsuspectin' stranger who thought he could best you."

Catherine laughed and went back to the

kitchen to help Bridget and Alice finish doing dishes. Maybe they'd plant the garden tomorrow morning. She'd need to go to the company store and buy seed. She put thoughts of Quincy leaving aside as she made a mental list that included peas, beans, sweet potato slips, cucumbers, squash and peppers.

When she went outside to check the rose and lilac bushes and the garden, she found the worms sitting on the porch. A full jar of wiggling, squirming creatures that looked exactly like her stomach felt. All nervous and crawly. She needed solitude and the river bank had always provided it. She'd fished with her father since she was big enough to walk. Perhaps she'd find answers to questions that plagued her soul. Besides, it would be a shame not to put them to use, especially when it had been months since she and her sisters had eaten catfish.

She carried them back inside and set them on the library table in the corner of the living room. She found Bridget sitting in a rocking chair in the bedroom working on the pink baby blanket.

"Think you ought to consider making a blue one?" Catherine asked as she shucked out of her clothes and found a pair of her father's oldest overalls. The ones she'd kept for occasions like fishing and digging six foot holes. They'd been washed since the night Ralph had the accident so there was no blood on them or dirt in the cuffs either.

"I'm not having a boy. I don't want one and God wouldn't punish me that bad. If it was a boy, it might be like Ralph. I want a daughter who looks like Momma and I'm going to name her Ella."

"Don't get your hopes up too high. I'm going fishing," Catherine said.

"I could eat some catfish, fried up crispy with some hush puppies, or maybe we could make a catfish chowder?" Bridget said.

"If I catch a stringer full we'll have both fried and chowder. We might even have enough for either dinner or supper tomorrow in the restaurant. We'll see," Catherine said.

"Take Momma's gun. You never know what kind of two legged varmints might be roaming around on the river," Bridget said.

"I won't need it. Tell Alice I've gone fishing. I expect she's out sketching somewhere?"

"Said she was going to check on the hawk she's been trying to get a good picture of," Bridget said.

Catherine had a bamboo pole and the jar of worms in her hands as she rounded the side of the hotel and headed toward the front yard.

Quincy fell into step with her.

"Where are you going?" She asked.

He still wore his overalls and flannel shirt and carried a pole he'd found in the tool shed.

"Fishin'. I borrowed a pole and I dug up the worms so I suppose it's all right?"

"It's a free country. You might ruin your reputation being seen with one of the crazy O'Shea women, you know."

"Could."

"You can't take fish with you on a train so if you catch anything, they're mine."

"Deal."

"And I'm not in the mood for talk."

"Me, neither."

"Then come on. You can drive."

"Drive?"

"Of course. I'm not walking the whole way to the river."

For a split second he wondered if that's where Ralph's body went. He didn't doubt for a moment that the man was dead. Someone of his ilk wouldn't stay away from his family that long. He would need their money and support to keep up his high dollar lifestyle.

Although he couldn't disprove a word of

what they said, he still had doubts about whether the O'Sheas were telling the whole truth and nothing but the truth. He was at the point where he was more than willing to chalk up his first failure. Anything to get out of Huttig and back home where he belonged. He had a yearning to sit in the study and have a long conversation with his father about the case and see if Albert Massey could find a hole Quincy hadn't seen. He hoped his mother, Martha, had a platter full of oatmeal raisin cookies ready when he walked through the front door. And he really wanted to go out to dinner with Elizabeth and tell her all about a red haired Irish girl he had trouble getting out of his mind.

"Want to bring the shovel and dig up the whole river bank?" She asked.

"Are you a mind reader?"

"No, but I bet it chaps you to have to leave unfinished business," she said.

"You'll never know how much." He shoved the poles into the car, letting the ends stick out the back window.

CHAPTER SEVEN

The sun set in a blaze of orange, bright salmon and yellow, the colors peeking through pine tree branches. The river flowed quietly, not filling its banks or in a hurry to get anywhere. A soft spring breeze moved the trees, but only slightly. A family of beavers sat on top of a pile of sticks but disappeared quickly into their underwater castle when they spied human beings. Ferns were showing new growth in dark shady recesses and the whole area smelled like spring.

Catherine had her hook baited and in the water before Quincy. She chose a familiar old stump and braced her back against it. Her father had sat in that very spot many times, his fishing pole steady on a forked branch, his hat pulled down over his eyes. She missed him right then more than ever. After he'd died there'd been very little time for mourning. There was a business to run, and funeral upon funeral to attend since Patrick wasn't the only person in Union County who'd succumbed to the flu. They'd scarcely gotten back on their feet when Ella took sick.

Catherine wished at that moment she was alone because she truly felt like weeping. Not that lady like, dabbing of the eyes crying. More like screaming at the sky and demanding an answer from God, while she sobbed until her eyes swelled shut and her throat was raw. But she couldn't give way to emotions while Quincy was baiting a fishing hook. He'd either try to walk on water to get away from her or else he'd attempt to console her. Either one was unacceptable.

Since she had to reign in her feelings about Quincy, she forced herself to remember good times she'd spent with her father. Like fishing in that very spot or what he'd said one of the first times he'd taken her along with him. She'd been a little red haired girl with braids hanging down her back and wore her oldest gingham dress. Momma said a girl didn't even belong on the bank of the river and she wasn't going to ruin a good school dress.

"Are you sleeping? Aren't you afraid you'll lose the fish?" Catherine asked her father all those years ago.

"I'm thinking. Fishing is for food, my child, but it's also for thinking," he'd answered.

Catherine wasn't so sure ten years later that she wanted to embrace her thoughts. She'd just as soon keep her eyes open and fish because every time she shut her eyes lately all she saw was Quincy, who was just as handsome in his working overalls and flannel shirt as in a three piece suit with his shoes polished to a shine.

Quincy got everything arranged and sat down on a log not five feet from her. "I've a confession. I lied to you," he said bluntly.

"You didn't grow up in Oklahoma did you?"

"Are you sure you're not a mind reader?" He asked.

"No, I can just spot a lie."

"I thought the Irish were gifted with words as in kissing the Blarney Stone and all that. I didn't know they were clairvoyant."

"You wanted my sympathy so maybe I'd tell you more about Ralph. You don't like being wrong and you sure don't like to go home empty handed. A dead body is better than failure, isn't it?"

"Guilty as charged," he said.

"Why are you telling me that you lied? You're leaving tomorrow and we'll never see each other again."

"It didn't set well with my conscience," he said.

"You've never lied before? Not even when you were a spy?"

"That wasn't true either."

"And the kiss? Was it to ferret information out of me also?"

"No, that was real enough."

Major's voice preceded him out of the darkness. Neither of them heard the rustle of someone approaching so when Major yelled they both jumped as if they'd been caught doing something immoral.

"Well, praise the Lord above. You came to your senses. I was worried you'd let her sneak off by herself. Body never knows what kind of varmints might be on the river banks."

"Major, it's good to see you again. Join us," Quincy said.

Well, that was convenient. Just what would you have said next if Major hadn't saved you? Catherine wondered.

"Can't. I was just joshing you, son. I didn't come down here to fish. I left my hat at the Black Swan and went back to get it and the sheriff come by. He said he had a message for you. Did you know his wife is from Huttig? They moved over to El Dorado when he got the sheriff job. Anyway, she had a hankering to come home and spend the night with her sister so he brought her and at the same time brought a message for you. It'll be layin' in the pigeon hole with your room number on it. He said he didn't want you to get on the north bound 'til you read it. And now since I see you two is busy I'm goin' on home."

"You don't have to leave," Quincy said. "Sit a spell. Maybe you'll bring us good luck."

"You got a pole hiding back there in the trees and just waitin' on an invitation?" Catherine asked.

"No, ma'am. I'm just out givin' Rowdy, my horse, some exercise. Truth be known I should be walkin' off too much food in a single day. A man who eats like that and don't work it all off will get fat. I can't afford to buy new overalls. Besides I'm going to visit with old man Walker on the way back home. He just lives a little ways on up the river. I brung two cigars. If we get to talkin' politics it could be a long night, 'specially if he gets me started on that danged communism stuff," Major chuckled.

"Too bad, we could have used another hook in the water if we're going to have fish chowder for dinner tomorrow," Catherine said.

"Would've brought it along if I'd knowed you had that in mind. Good-night," Major tipped his hat and disappeared into the darkness.

Catherine waited several minutes before she spoke. "I didn't tell you the whole truth, either."

The skin on the back of Quincy's neck crawled. He didn't realize until that very moment how much he wanted to be wrong; how much he was drawn to Catherine. She was about to tell everything and he didn't want to hear it. He had his mouth open about to tell her the report was finished and he had no intention of amending it even if it did produce results to make him a winner instead of a loser.

"There's another place on our property you haven't searched. We have a root cellar under the tool shed. At the back side, under where you found the shovels, there's a trap door leading down into it. Momma insisted Daddy make her one so she could keep turnips and potatoes all winter. You might want to take a look at it before you leave," she said.

"Will I find anything buried there?"

"Possibly. We buried Alice's cat down

there about ten years ago. She couldn't stand the idea of a wild animal digging up old Bootsy so Momma said we could have a funeral in the root cellar. We did it real proper. Lined a wood crate with an old pillow case, laid him out and had singing and praying over his dead carcass. Wept over him like he was royalty and then Momma made us cookies and milk for the wake. His bones are probably about a foot deep. I'm not sure if the wood crate rotted yet or not," she said.

"I think I can take a quick look and not disturb old Bootsy's grave." He didn't realize he'd been holding his breath until it all came out in a whoosh.

"Had you worried, didn't I?" Catherine asked.

"Not in the least."

"And that's another lie."

A bolt of lightning shot through the pine trees and the crack of thunder that followed startled both of them. They'd been so busy with their confessions they hadn't noticed dark clouds rolling toward them from the southwest.

Catherine gathered in her fishing line, wrapped it around the bamboo pole and set off in a fast walk toward the car. "You better be following me. We get more than our share of tornadoes in this area. They come out of the southwest most of the time and those clouds look mean enough to produce one."

When she looked back over her shoulder Quincy was so close she could see the whites of his eyes. They'd barely slammed both car doors when the rain started. Drops as big as hen eggs torpedoed out of the sky and hit the windows with ferocious force.

"March wind brings April showers," he recited.

"But it's still March," she protested. "It's coming in the back window. Throw those fishing poles out on the ground and roll up the windows. We can replace them. Water would damage the seats."

He obeyed her barked orders and then settled back into the driver's seat. "Hope it's not too muddy to get out of here."

"Not if you stop talking and get started," she said. There were two things that scared the bejesus out of Catherine. Thunder and lightning shared the number one spot. Tornadoes came in a close second.

The Model T refused to start. No matter how many times Quincy tried, he couldn't perform magic or even mumble curses evil enough to make the engine turn over. Finally, he slapped the steering wheel and glared at Catherine.

"Don't look at me like that. I'd rather be shoveling chicken manure than sitting in this car in a storm with you," she smarted off.

"Did you fill the gas tank recently?" He asked.

"You've been driving it more than we have. Did you fill the tank?"

Lightning split the sky and hit a tree not twenty feet behind them bringing it crashing down, the top landing in the river. Thunder loud enough to deafen folks in Little Rock followed. Catherine squealed like a mouse in a trap, covered her eyes with her hands and tried to curl up in a ball.

Quincy touched her shoulder. "Hey, it's just noise and the tree didn't hit us."

She straightened up but another lightning bolt flashed from the sky and crackled when it hit ground not ten feet in front of the car. The noise that followed in its wake scared her so badly that she buried her face in his shoulder. "Make it go away," she whispered.

He patted her. "I would if I could."

At that moment he could have asked her anything. She would have confessed to murders she'd never committed, told the whole story about Ralph's accident, even owned up to the time she stole a piece of penny candy from the Company store back when she was nine years old. If God was sending the storm to punish her for her wicked deeds, for wishing Ralph would be crushed beneath a train or die of the flu, even for covering up his death, then she'd repent. God had her attention.

At least until she looked up and Quincy kissed her. After that God had to sit in the back seat. The storm lasted through five kisses. She counted every one of them.

Finally he broke away and scooted a few inches from her. "It's over."

"The storm?" She asked more than a little bit embarrassed.

He tried the engine and it turned over immediately.

Catherine could have kicked the fickle thing. Sometimes modern inventions weren't worth what they'd replaced. A horse and buggy would have never had such a problem. The horse would have been glad to get them out of the situation and back home in a hurry. In which case, she would have missed the kisses and they were worth enduring a full blown tornado.

He was leaving tomorrow but Catherine was never promising to marry a man again who couldn't make her all fuzzy inside with his kisses. Ira hadn't created that kind of stir and she *would* have it if she ever gave her promise to another man.

"You didn't answer me. Are you saying the storm is over or the kissing?" She asked boldly.

"Both. How are we going to get out of here with that tree blocking us in?"

"We aren't. Not in this car. We'll have to walk home and leave the car for someone to rescue later. You up for a long walk in mud?"

He looked down at his work boots. "I'm glad I'm not wearing my good shoes."

"That's all you've got to say?"

Did those kisses mean nothing to him? Did men and women behave themselves like that in the bigger cities?

"I suppose it is. It's stopped raining. Ready to start walking?"

"What about all that . . . what was it?"

"It was two adult people enjoying a bit of sparking."

"With no consequences?"

"You got it, honey," he said hoarsely. No way in the devil was he about to tell her how his heart and soul were both on fire.

"Have it your way." She opened the door and set off toward home, tearing a rip in the seat of her father's worn overalls when she climbed across the tree blocking her way.

The silence surrounding them in the clean

night air was as deafening as the thunder claps earlier. She couldn't believe she'd let him kiss her like that. It's a wonder Ella's ghost wasn't sitting on her shoulder haunting her. If her father had been alive, he would have met them on the front porch, shotgun in hand and Quincy would have been a married man as soon as he could roust a preacher out of bed.

Married! Good God, she didn't want to be married to Quincy. A few kisses didn't ruin her reputation especially if no one ever knew they'd happened. Quincy wasn't the kiss and tell kind. His conscience had trouble lying to her. Besides she'd just learned the effects of a man on a woman. She sure didn't want to marry the first man who'd caused her to go weak in the knees. For all she knew Quincy could be lying about more than his upbringing. She brought her fingers to her lips to see if they were as hot as they felt. Lying or not, he could sure kiss.

She made plans as she walked. They'd come in through the back way and she'd allow him to cross their living room into the lobby of the hotel. Her sisters would be in their bedroom, hopefully sound asleep. Tomorrow she'd tell them the story of the storm and how the car wouldn't start and even throw in details about how she and Quincy had sparred over who did or did not fill up the gas tank. They'd ask Henry Matthis to suggest a couple of strong men from the mill who'd like to make an extra dollar or two to bring her car home. He'd be gone on the train by noon. The old adage said, 'out of sight, out of mind,' and in a week he'd just be another customer's name on the register book of the Black Swan Hotel.

Rather than her mother's sharp tongue haunting her as she trudged through mud, it was Ira's sweet gaunt face that appeared right over her left shoulder. He'd loved her and asked her to be there for him and she should still be mourning, not out kissing a stranger five times. Storm or no storm, it was more unforgivable than hiding Ralph's body.

They still weren't talking when they reached the back door of the hotel and she took him through their living room and into the lobby. She did close her eyes briefly and give thanks her sisters were already in the bedroom with the door closed. Hopefully, they'd slept through the noise and other than asking if she'd caught any fish, wouldn't even mention it the next morning.

"My message, please," he said.

She picked it out of the compartment and handed it to him.

He carried it up to his room.

She went to hers. She washed up and eased open the bedroom door. Two lamps burned brightly. Bridget looked up, questions on her face.

"So do I get Pappa's gun and demand he make an honest woman out of you?" Alice asked.

"We got caught in the storm. We thought the car was out of gas but it started right up when the storm passed. Lightning struck a tree and it fell right behind us so we couldn't drive home or we'd have been here a long time ago. We had to walk. I don't think that's enough to warrant a wedding," Catherine snapped.

"No, but what happened in the car might," Alice said.

"Maybe I'd better make a blue blanket for you," Bridget said.

"I'm going to bed. I've walked all the way home from the river. It's the middle of the night and I'm tired. I'm sure not in the mood for a confession or for scolding. Thank you for waiting up for me," Catherine said.

Bridget giggled.

Alice laughed aloud.

Catherine pulled the covers over her head.

Quincy lit a lamp and held the letter for a long time before he opened it. It was addressed in his father's firm handwriting and sealed with an M set in a glob of wax on the backside. That meant it was important and he'd be sent on another job with no time in between. Quincy had thought about a few weeks reprieve all the way back to the hotel. He longed for quiet evenings and no reports or a certain red haired woman's kisses that set his mind to desiring the impossible.

Finally, he broke the seal and read the words his father had written.

Dear son:

I got your telegram and will look for your full report by mail in the next few days. I would have sent this by same but we just finalized the plans today so I'm sending it by courier to the sheriff in El Dorado. I think it will cause less stir than if I sent the courier all the way into Huttig or if I called on the telephone. Can't expect to tell anything on one of those that you don't want repeated in an hour. A man isn't fired from his job by a fancy courier so you can expect a phone call at the Black Swan tomorrow morning in which you will be fired. I'm hoping the news will spread over town rapidly. We need for everyone to know that you've been fired. You are to go on with your plans and leave the Black Swan and check into the Commericial.

You are not coming home right now. After that, of course we will put you back in your old job and if you get this done satisfactorily, I promise two weeks vacation.

He laid his head on the window sill and groaned. It was far worse than he'd imagined. He would be leaving the Black Swan but staying in Huttig. His heart fell somewhere between the floor and hell.

He read the rest of the letter.

His orders were to check into the Commercial for a week. After that there would be a company house vacated for him. He would take the news with anger and march right into the mill to ask for a job. With the war ending, men were coming home in droves, needing work, but with no war machine to feed, jobs were getting scarcer by the hour. There was dissention at the mill; a strike on the horizon. Quincy's new job was to discover those wanting trouble and prevent a disaster.

So for all intents and purposes, Quincy

had just been fired from his detective job for failure to settle Ralph's whereabouts, whether living or dead. The Contiellos had pull in high places. He'd lost his job for failure to turn up their son. That was the story at least.

Because of his education in business and finance, the mill had hired him, put him in an office and his job was to oversee production. His actual job was to take information to the owner each evening. He would keep his ears and eyes open and hopefully, the downsizing of personnel wouldn't create a small war in Huttig.

He read the letter again and a third time. Two months at the most, his father promised.

"Two months of living in a saw mill house and pretending. Right here in the town with Catherine and after tonight. Lord, what was I thinking? She's going to spit in my face when she finds out. Major, you don't have to worry about me out running the up and coming bride crop. My father just took care of that," Quincy said out loud.

He read the last paragraph one more time.

I'm sending Elizabeth. She'll be back from an assignment in Kansas City tomorrow. She will be your sweet little wife who will be living with you in your company house. She's a professional and if the mill wives know anything, she'll get the information out of them in record time. I know you two are great friends so it won't be an imposition for you to pretend to be her husband. Oh, the house has two bedrooms so you don't have to share. That's a joke, my son. In case you didn't know, she is recently engaged to another detective. He's not too happy with this assignment, but you two have worked together successfully in the past and I need this upheaval settled quickly. Sending basic furniture and things you'll need by train in the morning. It should be there by the time Elizabeth arrives. She'll be on the noon train from Little Rock next Monday. Your mother sends her love. She'll make those cookies you love when you finish this job. Two months and you can have a two week break. You have my word.

"I don't want a break in two months. I want it now. I want to take Catherine a bouquet and squire her around town. I want to get to know her better. I dang sure don't want to be married to Elizabeth right here in Huttig. Catherine is going to think I'm the biggest cad on the face of the earth and

I won't be able to explain a single thing to her," he groaned aloud.

CHAPTER EIGHT

Mabel Matthis picked her way around mud holes and wet grass to the Black Swan. Yes, ma'am, she was carrying gossip to the O'Shea girls and could hardly wait to see the look on Catherine's face when it was delivered. So Miss Hoity Toity Catherine O'Shea thought she was too good for one of the Matthis boys, did she? Well, she was getting her comeuppance, now wasn't she? First Ira died in the war. Then Quincy arrived in Huttig hunting for Ralph. There were several young women in town who'd thought he was a good catch but they'd all kept their distance once they learned Catherine might be interested. Even if single men, especially good looking ones with a prestigious job, were scarcer than hen's teeth, they'd given Catherine first chance since she'd recently lost Ira, not to mention both her parents within six months.

So it was with light steps that Mabel

pranced across the lawn in her Sunday best dress, a nice navy blue serge with white collar and cuffs. Those O'Shea girls might not respect the dead but Mabel did and she'd be wearing dark colors for her family and friends a whole year. Anyone with a lick of sense would think the O'Shea girls would be wearing black for at least six months but they thought they were above common mourning decency. Well, after today they'd see right quick that they weren't perfect, either. They made mistakes; big ones, and she was bringing the news right to them.

Business was slower than usual so there were only a few people in the hotel dining room when Mabel arrived. She sat with two other women from her church and shared the information in hushed whispers that she'd garnered from the preacher's wife the day before.

"Oh my, now isn't that a shame," Annabel clucked.

"It's a good thing Ella ain't alive to see all this disgrace. She would have sent Bridget back home where she belongs with a good stiff lecture about her wedding vows. And she'd have set Catherine straight, I'm here to tell you," Eula joined in.

"Now I don't know about Bridget. Can't see Ella puttin' up with a man bein' downright mean to one of her girls but I know she'd have put Catherine on the straight and narrow," Annabel said.

Alice brought coffee and tea and all three women went silent. "And how are you ladies today?" She asked.

"Fine, just fine. Where is Catherine?" Mabel asked. Be danged if she'd give out her news and let Alice carry it to the kitchen.

"She's gone to the Company store for supplies. I expect she'll be back soon. You want to talk to her or can I give her a message?"

"Oh, it's nothing. Just something I wanted to share with her," Mabel smiled. "That ham sure smells good. I've been lookin' forward to having dinner here all morning. Just got the last of my washin' on the line. Sure hope it don't rain."

"Sun is out bright. Doesn't look like rain to me. I'll be back in a minute with your plates," Alice said.

Catherine put in a standard weekly order for flour, sugar, salt, lard, a hundred pound sack of potatoes, half a bushel each of sweet potatoes and carrots, and fifty pounds of cornmeal. She fingered the flannel as she passed the fabric table and thought of buying a few yards for diapers. On second thought, that wouldn't be wise. Wait until the divorce was granted. The Contiello family would fight it to the end if they knew a grandchild was on the way.

"Well, hello, Catherine. I was in the stock room trying to figure out where to put a new load of fabric and didn't hear you. How are things at the Black Swan?" Minnie, the store manager's wife, called from halfway across the store as she approached in long strides. Minnie was even taller than Catherine and heavier by thirty pounds. She wore her dark hair in a new fashionable bob that looked good with her round face.

"Just fine. We still aren't up to full with guests but the flu scare is barely past and the Commercial isn't running at capacity either. I expect it has something to do with the mill not running day and night. Restaurant is doing fine. Guess people will venture out to eat when they're afraid to sleep in a bed for fear of getting the flu."

"That they will," Minnie said. "Of course, your good cooking will bring them out of the woodwork, flu or not."

"Thank you. What's going on around here? I haven't been by in a couple of weeks now."

"Did you hear that they've got a new supervisor over at the mill?"

"Oh?" Catherine could care less about who worked at the mill. Even if it did provide the town with a living, the inner parts of the business didn't matter to her. Now if they shut the mill down, that might be worthy of her consideration. Without the mill, Huttig would soon be a ghost town. Her business as well as the rest of the hotels, dining places and stores in town wouldn't last long without people to support them.

"Yes, that man that stayed at the Black Swan," Minnie said.

"Jed Tanner. I thought he was a newspaper man."

"No, that's not his name. Mr. Tanner left town. He tried his best to get us to tell him something about Ralph but we can't tell what we don't know. I heard Ralph was mean to Bridget. Is that the truth?"

"Yes, it is. I'm glad she's back home," Catherine said.

"Well, the day Tommy thinks he can lay a hand on me in a mean way is the day I'll plant his sorry carcass six feet down and not shed a tear. Someday women won't have to put up with such things," Minnie declared.

"Let's hope we live to see that day."

"Oh, about that supervisor. He came in and bought up a bunch of groceries to be delivered to the old Oldham house. That last one on the way to Felsenthal. About half a mile from the mill."

"I know where it is. Momma went there to take care of Mrs. Oldham and brought the flu home with her."

"I'm so sorry about that. Ella was a good woman. She and your father are missed terribly. They were some of the first folks to build here, I understand. I heard the Oldham daughters cleaned out the house and the mill gave it to the new supervisor," Minnie said.

Catherine looked at the pale green calico. Bridget could make a nice blouse from that, one that would match her new chambray overalls she'd ordered from the Sears catalog. She'd said that she would wear the loose fitting overalls as long as she could to cover her condition.

"Momma was a kind soul. We miss her everyday. Sometimes I think I need to run to the kitchen and tell Momma something I heard and then I realize she's gone. I suppose it will be like that for a long time. I'd like four yards of this," Catherine said.

Minnie picked up the bolt of fabric and carried it to the cutting table. "In a mood to sew, are you?"

"No, but Bridget ordered new overalls and

this will make a pretty blouse to go with them. She don't know it but she's in the mood to sew," Catherine said.

Minnie laughed.

Catherine joined her, the heavy mood replaced by something as simple as a joke.

"Oh here comes that new supervisor. You already know him. He stayed at the Swan. Come here to check on Ralph. You'll remember him when you see him. Lord, how could a woman not remember him? He gives all of us, married and single alike, the vapors." Minnie whispered.

Catherine's heart skipped two beats then set ahead with a full head of steam. Quincy was supposed to be back in Little Rock or off doing whatever detectives did when they weren't investigating missing men. He'd left the Swan eight days ago, settled up his bill and walked out the front door without so much as an acknowledgement of those five kisses. *He* was the new supervisor at the mill? Good God in Heaven, what had happened in the last week?

"Good day, Minnie, I'd like you to meet my wife, Elizabeth. Please let her charge whatever she needs on my account," Quincy said.

"I'm pleased to make your acquaintance and the way this man likes to eat, I'm sure

I'll be in here often. Oh, darlin' look at this material. Don't you think it would make lovely kitchen curtains? I'll have to measure the windows and come back later," Elizabeth said.

"Want me to put the bolt aside until you do?" Minnie asked.

"That would be lovely. I promise I'll be back tomorrow morning at the latest," Elizabeth said.

They kept talking but it was nothing but a low buzz in Catherine's aching heart. If only the floor could open up and swallow her whole so she didn't have to look at Quincy. She began to ease toward the front door. Hopefully, she could stay hidden behind the tables until she could make a dash outside.

He was married! And he'd kissed her, at two different times, the last time more than once, so it couldn't be a happening of the moment. Catherine didn't want to see Quincy but curiosity made her peek at Elizabeth.

She was lovely, Catherine had to give her that. A short little blond haired lady with her hair pinned back in a chaste bun at the nape of her neck. A nice navy blue serge tunic dress with a loose panel waist front decorated with the ever-popular military braid. Catherine had seen the same dress in the Sear's catalog and remembered it sold for more than sixteen dollars. Evidently detectives made more money than saw mill workers. Elizabeth had better make it last a long time, because the days when she could spend that kind of money were long gone.

"Oh, let me introduce you to Catherine. Where are you?" Minnie looked across the fabric table to find Catherine missing.

"I'm right here. I was looking at buttons," Catherine said. She'd been caught. The only thing she could do was meet the situation head on with as much grace as she could muster up from her shattered pride. Good God, she had fallen for a married man!

"Well, come and meet Mrs. Massey. You already know Mr. Massey. He stayed at your hotel, remember?" Minnie said.

"Hello, Mr. Massey. I wasn't aware you were still in town," Catherine said.

"New job," Quincy said hoarsely. "This is my wife, Elizabeth. We will be living in the Oldham place. You'll have to visit when you have time."

When pigs fly and cows sprout halos, you absolute worthless piece of garbage. God, what were you thinking? Does this woman know how you behave when you are away from her?

Catherine extended her hand to Elizabeth.

"And you'll have to bring Mrs. Massey to the hotel for supper some night."

Catherine had expected a limp shake, one that said the woman was a sweet piece of fluff without a backbone. She got a surprise when Elizabeth shook her hand firmly and held it for a moment.

"I'm glad to meet you. Quincy has done nothing but brag about the food at your hotel. Please call me Elizabeth, darlin'. You and Minnie are my first friends in Huttig. I'm thinking that we might even come to your dining room tonight for supper since I won't have time to get things ready to cook this fast."

She was as pretty as one of those kewpie dolls from the carnival that came through town once a year. A sweet little round face, big, innocent blue eyes, and tiny little hands. Everything but her handshake said she was a feminine little thing in need of protection.

Quincy looked embarrassed and miserable, as well he should.

"If you have that fabric cut, I'll be on my way," Catherine said.

"I guess you hadn't heard that I was fired from the detective agency," Quincy said. "I liked this area so I walked into the saw mill and they hired me on the spot. I was really quite fortunate."

"Yes, he was and I'm so glad to be moving out of the big city. I think I'll like Huttig. It reminds me of home. I grew up in Oklahoma. Out around Tonkawa," Elizabeth said.

Catherine nodded. She'd heard that story before. Was it the real truth after all?

"Good luck with your new job and you with your new home." Catherine's voice sounded hollow even to her own ears, but she'd be staked out on an ant hill before she let that rascal of a man know how just being in his presence affected her.

"Thank you and I'll be looking forward to spending more time with you," Elizabeth said.

Not if I can help it, Catherine thought as she picked up her fabric and marched out of the store.

She was on the edge of having an all out temper fit by the time she got back to the hotel and parked the car. She all but stormed into the kitchen past the patrons who'd smiled and mumbled things about the weather and good food. She managed a weak, fake smile and put on an act that fooled them but not her sisters. By the time she'd tied an apron around the waist of her plain blue work dress, and picked up the

143

coffee pot and tea pitcher, Alice and Bridget were both at her side.

"What's the matter with you? You look like you could kill someone," Alice said.

"Starting with Quincy," Catherine said.

"I thought he was gone." Bridget said.

"No, he got fired for not figuring out Ralph's whereabouts. They hired him the next day at the mill. Don't you think that's strange since the work load is falling and there's talk of layin' men off. He just walks in there and gets a job. Then they give him the Oldham house when there's others been waiting on a Company house for months. That's not going to help him make friends," Alice said.

"Why didn't you tell me?" Catherine asked.

"Because you were at the store buying supplies," Alice answered.

Bridget came to her defense. "She was just now telling me. That's what everyone is talking about. I'm surprised we didn't hear it before now. It's been a whole week and no one even mentioned it at church yesterday."

Catherine moaned. "That's because they all thought there was something going on between him and me. God, I'm ruined."

"I offered to dust off Papa's shot gun that night of the storm but you wouldn't have no part of it," Alice reminded her.

Bridget pushed back a strand of strawberry blond hair and went back to work. "Just hold your head up and forget it. So he got fired. At least he didn't find Ralph. So he kissed you. Who cares? Lots of boys kissed me before Ralph."

Alice was suddenly more interested in that than Quincy. "How many?"

Bridget shrugged her shoulders. "A dozen maybe."

"Good lord," Catherine said.

"Yes, the Lord is very good and Momma would have your hide for using His name in vain," Bridget reminded her.

"And yours for kissing a dozen boys," Catherine said. "Oh, and Quincy . . . Mr. Massey . . . is married. Her name is Elizabeth and I just met her."

Bridget and Alice both stared at her as she pushed the door open into the dining room.

"None of the dozen were married, I promise," Bridget whispered.

Alice just smiled and filled a platter with hot rolls.

Catherine made her way around the tables, filling coffee cups and tea glasses. Stopping to visit with one group or another. Talking about the weather. Hoping the flu epidemic was really over. Garnering gossip about who was sick, who'd had a baby in the past few days, who'd finally gotten a company house. If the fish were biting and when they might offer fried catfish on the menu. The sermon the previous day at the Methodist Church, the Baptist church or the one down on the corner where they prayed really loud. Normal conversation on any given day at the hotel.

"Well, Catherine, I'm so glad you got back," Mabel smiled sweetly when Catherine finally got to her table.

"Had to go for supplies. Wouldn't last long without flour and sugar," Catherine said.

Mabel patted the fourth chair at her table. "Have a seat here for a few minutes."

Catherine did a quick scan. Everyone appeared to be in good shape. She pulled out the chair and sat down. "What's on your mind?"

"That Quincy Massey. That's what's on my mind. He was courtin' you while he lived here. That's not socially acceptable and you know it."

Catherine swallowed hard to keep from choking. "He was a friendly man but I wouldn't say he was courtin' me by any means."

Let that news get out and Catherine

would have a tainted reputation in the whole county, not just Huttig. One O'Shea would be divorced. One ruined. One a little light in the mental area. Thank goodness Momma and Papa weren't alive to see such things.

"Oh, I do think he was courtin' you and now we find out that he's married. He's bringing his wife to Huttig. It's a disgrace the way he acted when she wasn't with him. How does that make you feel?" Mabel asked.

Catherine put on her best smile. "Like I said he never one time asked if he could court me, nor did he give me the impression he wanted to court me. And I met his sweet little wife today at the company store. There's a possibility she'll be having supper with us tonight right here at the Swan since she doesn't have things arranged in her new little house. Maybe you and Henry would like to come on over for supper and meet her," Catherine lowered her voice to a mere whisper. "Do you think he'd be bringing his wife here of all places if he'd been courtin' me? I think not. He'd be keeping her away from here for fear I'd let the cat out of the bag. And what with Henry working at the mill still, it might not be a good idea for you to be spreading such gossip around

147

about the new supervisor. It might not bode well for his job."

Mabel blanched.

"Guess you were wrong, Mabel. I'd heard Mr. Massey might be interested in Catherine, also. Guess we old busy bodies just wanted you to find a man and be happy, Catherine. We thought he might be a good catch but we didn't know he was already caught. Guess we were seein' things that we wanted to see rather than what was there to see," Eula said.

Mabel regained a little color. "Yes, that's it."

"Finding a man doesn't always make a woman happy. Look at Bridget," Catherine said.

Annabel looked up. "You said a mouth full there. My man ever lays a hand on me and even though I'm fifty years old he'll pay for it. I'll wait 'til he's asleep and sew him up in the bed sheet he's layin' on and honey I'll take the business end of a shovel to him. I'll beat him until he straightens up or until he's a dead man. Either way he'd better enjoy his fit while he's havin' it because it'll be the first and last. Women folks has got to take matters into their own hands, that's what I say. That's what Bridget should have done to Ralph. Bet she wishes she had shown him how a beatin' feels now that he's run off with some floozie and she'll never get the chance to do it."

"I'm sure she does. I see a coffee cup empty. Nice chatting with you ladies," Catherine said.

She managed to get through the dinner rush without falling apart but when it was over she gave in to an emotional upheaval. She went to her bedroom, flung herself across the bed and glared at the ceiling as if it had a hole in it providing a straight shot into heaven. Nothing made a bit of sense.

Alice painted.

Bridget picked up her knitting and settled into a rocking chair.

Both gave Catherine room to work out her demons. She'd talk when she got ready. There was that much Ella bred into her. When their mother was in a tizz about something, she needed time to work it out before they talked about it. All three girls had learned early on to give her space when she was angry.

After more than an hour of replaying every word, every nuance, every single kiss several times, Catherine finally sat up. "Okay, Bridget, you might be the youngest of us, but you've got the most experience. Did you ever kiss a man and your knees go limp?"

Bridget laid the knitting aside and shook her head. "No, I did not. Kissed some boys who were downright nasty. Remember Matthew Riddly. I didn't know he had a chaw in his mouth and he kissed me. That was absolutely horrid. Then I kissed some that were nice. John Adler told me I was the most beautiful woman on the face of the whole earth and then he kissed me. It was right nice. He'd been eating peppermint. Ralph's were pleasant. Even when we . . ." she stammered. Even with sisters, there were things women didn't discuss.

"What?" Alice asked.

"Oh, hell, if women are ever going to have rights, we've got to be able to talk about things. I imagine men folks can say whatever they please when us women aren't around but I might blush," Bridget said.

"Go on, we'll forgive your face going crimson," Alice said.

"It wasn't all bad, you know. He could be very nice when he wanted to be and sometimes he could kiss very well."

"But his kisses didn't make your legs go all weak and your heart pound like it was trying to break free of your chest?" Catherine asked.

"Good lord, no!" Bridget was aghast.

"Not one time when anyone of those fellows kissed you did you have the urge to do more than just kiss?" Catherine asked.

"Most of the time I didn't even like the kisses. They seemed to enjoy it so I endured them," she said.

"Hmmmm," Catherine put her finger over her mouth and drew her eyes down.

"Why'd you marry him then?" Alice asked.

"Because I didn't want to be an old maid."

"Thank you for your honesty," Catherine said. "I'm going to make two more coconut pies. I've got a feeling there'll be a supper rush tonight because I told Mabel that Quincy was bringing his wife in for supper. She won't let her skirt tail touch her fanny until she's out there spreading that bit of news. We'll have a full house and folks waiting in the lobby. Miz Elizabeth Massey will think we're puttin' on a party for her. Oh, and there's a length of pretty calico on the sofa for you, Bridget. I thought you could make a blouse to go with your new overalls."

"Thank you. You say Quincy is bringing his wife? Why would he do that? Here? If she finds out how he looks at you, she's going to be mad."

"Not as mad as she's going to be when she sees how Catherine looks at him," Alice said.

"Oh, both of you hush. I'm a grown

woman. I'm so angry at that man he'd better be dodging my looks. They could probably kill him grave yard dead," Catherine said.

"Well, I'm glad she's coming to the hotel. We can meet her. Maybe we'll be friends," Alice said.

Catherine shot her a look meant to fry such a notion out of her empty head.

Alice cocked her head to one side and smiled impishly.

CHAPTER NINE

Mabel had done a fine job of spreading the news. The dining room was full and the lobby was crowded with folks waiting for a table. Catherine, Bridget and Alice barely kept up. At six o'clock when Quincy and Elizabeth arrived the evening had turned into a 'welcome to Huttig' party. Everyone who had a husband, brother, nephew or boyfriend working at the mill, as well as those who were just plain curious were in attendance, waiting for a few words with the new supervisor and his lovely wife.

Quincy and Elizabeth were shuffled from one group to another in the lobby, made welcome and invitations to dinners extended. Elizabeth was elated with the warmth and friendliness of the small town but still kept her fingers crossed that the assignment might be over in much less than two months.

In the middle of the whole thing, eight

men arrived to check into the hotel for two days. Catherine left a hectic kitchen and showed them to their rooms, barely taking time to smile at Elizabeth and shoot Quincy a 'drop graveyard dead' look.

The first setting in the dining room finished eating and the second filtered in to take their places but the tables filled up before the Masseys were seated. That gave the ones who'd been eating time to meet, greet, invite and be known. Catherine could care less about who'd met the lovely little Elizabeth or shaken hands with the liar, Quincy. She just wanted the evening to be over with and life to get back to the way it was before Quincy arrived on her front porch.

The new lodgers tossed their belongings in rooms and followed her back to the lobby to see what all the fuss was about, hoping that they'd hear something about jobs as they waited for their turn to eat. As people ate and left, the lobby cleared out leaving a young couple and a few stragglers. No one had mentioned work; they'd been too busy welcoming the Masseys. Finally, one of the strangers held his hand out toward Quincy. "I'm Harold Bigsby. Just got out of the service and heard they might be hiring at the mill. Me and my buddies have come to see about work."

Quincy shook his hand. "I don't think they're hiring but you could go talk to them. Never know until you ask."

Another shook hands with Quincy. "I'm Baxter Wright. This place always this busy?"

"Pleased to meet you. No, it's busy but not usually this much. You'll enjoy the food and the rooms are clean," Quincy said.

Elizabeth left a group of older women and joined Quincy. "I believe they are about to find us a spot. This is nice, darlin'. Folks are so friendly."

"My wife, Elizabeth. This is Harold and this is Baxter. They've come to town hunting for work." He made introductions.

"Pleased to meet you. Good luck on finding a job," she said.

Catherine motioned to them and led them to a table. "Tea or coffee?"

"Tea for me. Coffee for Quincy. The ham smells lovely."

"I hope you like it," Catherine said sweetly. Momma said southern women behaved themselves with dignity. At that moment, she would have liked to toss dignity out with the dish water and snatch all the hair from Quincy's head.

You'd still be attracted to him if he was bald. You are stupid, stupid, stupid, Catherine Elvira

O'Shea. First of all he was a detective investigating Ralph's disappearance so that makes him off limits. Second, he's married so that dang sure takes him off the market. Why do I want what I cannot ever have?

Elizabeth reached out and grabbed her hand as she went by. "I believe there is something on my napkin. Would you check please?"

Catherine couldn't see a thing but she leaned down to check it closer. It was folded perfectly, ironed crisply, no stains.

Elizabeth pointed to an inside corner. "Right there."

Catherine leaned so close that her ear was barely an inch from Elizabeth's lips.

"Darlin' believe nothing you hear and only half of what you see," she whispered softly.

Catherine straightened her back, not sure if she'd heard right or understood if she did. "What?"

"Oh, silly me, it must have been a gnat flying around. I'm just hungry and seeing things. I'm so sorry to have bothered you," Elizabeth said.

Catherine glanced at Quincy. Misery was etched into his face but that was his comeuppance for not telling her he was married. Elizabeth was all bubbly and smiling at everyone who stopped by their table for a few words. Poor dear was even more stupid than Catherine imagined herself to be. Maybe she had air for brains like Alice and Quincy didn't know it until after he'd married her.

It doesn't matter. He did and that's the end of that. There's absolutely no excuse for a man kissing another woman when he's already married.

She was still puzzled when she carried out their supper. What on earth was Elizabeth talking about? And why would she tell Catherine anything at all? She set their plates in front of them and Elizabeth slyly dropped a note in her apron pocket.

What had started out as a dreaded evening was turning into a complete mystery. First the woman tells her a riddle and then she very slickly put something in Catherine's pocket. Most likely it was a note telling her that Quincy had 'fessed up and Catherine was walking on thin ice.

"I don't think I could handle too many evenings like this," Bridget said when Catherine made another pass through the kitchen.

"I'm glad I made extra pies," Catherine said.

"Want me to put some arsenic in that woman's dessert?" Bridget asked.

"No, something isn't right out there."

"What's not right is that she and Quincy ain't married and they're going to be living together. That's what ain't right," Alice said.

Catherine's brow wrinkled and her eyebrows knit together over dark green eyes. "What?"

Alice shrugged. "Don't ask me how I know. I just do."

"You are being silly. Of course, they're married. If they weren't they'd be living in sin."

Don't believe anything you hear and only half of what you see.

Catherine pulled the paper from her pocket. Instead of threatening to slit Catherine's throat if she ever saw her with Quincy, it simply said:

Invite me over in the morning.

The whole world was upside down and inside out. Had Quincy married a crazy woman? That question could be answered easily enough if she did indeed invite Elizabeth to the hotel the next morning. Or it could be that she was a real lady and didn't hang her dirty laundry on the line for the whole town to see. Worse yet, it might be that Elizabeth was biding her time and was bringing more than an argument to the Black Swan.

Catherine balanced the coffee pot and two dessert plates with a slice of pie on a tray. The room wasn't as crowded as it had been all evening but it was still an obstacle course to get from the kitchen to the Massey's table. Quincy reached for a hot roll at the same time she set the china pie plate beside his coffee cup. The brush of his fingertips across her wrist set her to wanting the impossible again. Life was not fair. First Ira died. Even though there was no passion, they could have been a good couple. Her father died and her mother. Now she'd fallen for a man who could never know about Ralph and was married to boot.

"These yams are simply delicious. And that coconut pie, oh my, I wish I could get meringue to set up like that. What's your secret?" Elizabeth asked.

"Cream of tartar. Why don't you come over tomorrow morning and I'll show you how to make it? We make chocolate pies on Tuesdays," Catherine said.

"I'll look forward to it. Quincy goes to work at eight. Is that too early?"

"No, we'll be in the kitchen by then. Pot roast isn't worth eating unless it's cooked four hours," Catherine said.

Elizabeth laid her hand on Quincy's. "Is that all right with you, darlin'?"

"Of course. If you can learn to make chocolate pies like the O'Shea ladies, it will be time well spent," Quincy said.

By the time they finished the clean up and left the eight guests in the lobby talking about the prospects of jobs, all three of the ladies were worn to a frazzle. Bridget didn't even stop in the living room but went straight to her bedroom and slipped out of her dress and into a nightgown. She was asleep five minutes after she wiggled out a nest in the feather bed. Alice didn't even bother to wiggle; her eyes were shut in five seconds.

Catherine hadn't had time to mention the upcoming visit to her sisters. First of all she wanted alone time to process the idea of being a friend to Quincy's wife. Something definitely was not right even if she couldn't put her finger on it. Quincy acted like the loving husband but his face portrayed something different. Elizabeth was giggly and sweet but it never reached her blue eyes.

She sat in a rocking chair and watched the rising moon. Shaped like the cutout on the old outhouse down at the back of the lot, it took its own lazy time. She pulled her long legs up and wrapped her arms around them, keeping the motion of the chair going by leaning forward and back every few minutes. Long after midnight, when Bridget and Alice were both snoring so soft it sounded like the purrs of kittens, she forced herself to go to bed. She slept fitfully, and morning took a long time to arrive.

As was normal, their eight guests made up the breakfast crowd. Catherine served sausage gravy and biscuits, fried eggs, grits and pancakes. She wondered if Ira would have sat so ramrod straight had he come home from the war. When he'd left he'd been gangly, long arms and legs that he wasn't quite sure what to do with when he sat in a kitchen chair. Momma had said he'd muscle up as he got older but neither of his parents had a spare ounce of muscle or fat on them.

"Miss Catherine, this is wonderful food. When we was over there across the waters we missed good home cooking. We used to talk about what we'd be eatin' if we was home that night. It brought us comfort. Most of the time, it just made us so homesick we could cry like little girls. I wouldn't mind eatin' here all the time if we get hired on at the mill," Baxter said.

"I don't want to be the bearer of bad news but I don't think they're hiring. I heard they were getting ready to lay off a bunch of local men," Catherine said.

"Anything else in this town a man could work at?"

"Not much. The Company owns the Commercial Hotel and the main store in town. The whole place was built to accommodate the mill men about fifteen or sixteen years ago. Eleven miles on down the road in Union Parish, Louisiana there's a town called Marion. I heard the railroad might be hiring. Don't know about the saw mills down in that area. Where ya'll from?"

"We all hail from around Memphis, Tennessee. Work is scarce in most areas. Thousands of us coming home and the war all but over with. We just thought we'd use our last dollars on a trip down here when we heard there was work in the big pine area," Baxter said.

"I'm sorry the news couldn't be better, but they did hire a supervisor last week so maybe things are picking up after all. It won't do a bit of harm to check since you're already here." Catherine headed back toward the kitchen.

"If we get on with the mill, would you be interested in taking a walk with me some evening?" Baxter asked.

She stopped dead in her tracks. What had

they heard the night before? That she was one of those loose women?

"I never take walks with customers. It could cause talk," she said.

"Then if I get on at the mill, I'll move out," Baxter smiled brightly.

"Move out. Wait six months and then come ask me." She attempted to make light of the situation.

"It'll be well worth the wait," Baxter said.

Catherine escaped through the door and leaned against it. Bridget was busy washing dishes and Alice stirring chocolate pudding for the pies. If only life could go back a year. She'd put Bridget in a convent, send her parents off to some exotic island where the flu had no chance of survival, and turn down Ira's proposal.

A gentle knock on the opposite side of the door startled her. Surely Baxter hadn't followed her into the kitchen, a woman's sanctuary. She eased the door open a crack and was only mildly shocked when Elizabeth's blue eyes stared up at her.

"You did say eight was fine?" She asked.

Catherine slung the door open. "I'm sorry. I thought you might be . . . oh, it doesn't matter. Come on in. Alice is making pudding now for the pies. We'll get started on the crust so it will be out of the oven when the pudding is cooled."

She turned to her sisters and said, "I forgot to mention last night, I invited Elizabeth over to show her our secrets on making pies. She wants to make meringue that stands up real high." She talked too fast and said too many words when she was nervous. She clamped her mouth shut, determined that Quincy's wife was not going to make her jittery.

"And you are Bridget?" Elizabeth nodded toward the younger sister in overalls. Elizabeth would have certainly brought hers if she hadn't feared she'd be ostracized for wearing them, but there was the little fact that Quincy was her husband for the next couple of months and he hated them.

"And you'd be Alice?" Elizabeth had heard about Alice. Not so much from Quincy, who'd sworn the woman was not a feather brain but just used the excuse to do and say what she wanted, but from a couple of the ladies who'd whispered gossip into her ear the previous evening.

"Glad to meet you both," she said.

"We're glad you could come by. Ain't much of a secret to making meringue. Just add enough sugar and beat the devil out of it," Alice said.

Elizabeth turned to Catherine. "Well, I'm

anxious to learn. Could I possibly trouble you to use your bathroom before we start?"

"Of course. I'll show you where it is," Catherine said.

She led Elizabeth through the lobby. For some reason the wall paper looked shabby to her that day. She made a mental note to ask Minnie to see the paper book next time she was in the store. Maybe she'd ask Alice and Bridget what they thought of something with yellow cabbage roses for both the lobby and the dining room. Something to bring sunshine inside even when it was dreary outside.

She opened the door into their living quarters and stood back to let Elizabeth go ahead of her. "Momma insisted on us having our own place when the hotel was built. So we have a living room and two bedrooms back here. Papa put indoor plumbing in a few years ago. The bathroom is straight ahead."

"It's a lovely room. I like the wall paper. Always have loved daisies. The yellow woodwork is a nice touch. It looks so cheerful. The house we have needs new paper but I'm not so sure I'm going to get into that job just yet. I plan to make curtains, though." Elizabeth grabbed her arm and pulled her into the bathroom, shutting the door firmly behind them.

Catherine was speechless. Why on earth would the woman want her to come in such tight quarters with her? And the toilet of all places. They weren't best friends in the second grade, for great pity's sake.

Elizabeth leaned into the mirror hanging on the wall above the sink and using her fingers brushed a few errant blond hairs back into the tight little bun. "Can anyone hear us in here?" She whispered.

"I don't think so," Catherine said. The cat and mouse mystery stuff was about to fry her nerves.

"Then listen carefully and let me talk. I'm going out on a big limb to even tell you what I'm about to, so you've got to promise me that what I say will never leave this room. That means you can't even tell your sisters. Understood?"

Catherine nodded.

"Okay, I've been friends with Quincy all my life. My mother and his are sisters. That makes us first cousins."

Catherine's green eyes bulged.

"We are not married. I was an actress and am now a detective just like he is. We've had lots of assignments together but this is possibly my last one. He has no idea I'm telling you this and if you say or do one thing to let him know, I'll swear you are lying. I saw the way he looked at you yesterday and I knew. Don't ask me why and I'm not asking you any questions about what went on while he was here on the Contiello case. I'm engaged and I have always had a soft heart for him. So anyway, bear with us for the next two months, and then we'll be gone. After that, the story can be that I took the flu or that I ran away with a band of gypsies. It won't matter and he'll be free to do whatever he wants."

At that moment, every emotion possible rattled around in Catherine like beans in a glass pickle jar. She shook her head to be sure she was awake and not dreaming.

"But what . . ." she stammered.

"No questions. Just believe me and don't ever mention this to anyone. Remember, 'Don't believe anything you hear and only half of what you see.' Two months will pass quickly."

"That depends," Catherine finally found her tongue.

"Quincy has no idea I'm telling you this and if he found out he'd be so mad my life would be miserable the next few weeks. Today I'm a homemaker and Quincy is my husband. On the last mission I was an English princess and he was my cousin act-ing as my chaperone. That's all I'm telling you, Miss O'Shea. That and please don't be looking at him like you could have him for breakfast in my presence or I will be forced to make a big scene. Now let's go make pies."

"But I don't even know how I feel . . ."

"I think you do. Now about those pies?"

"This is going to take a while for me to sort out, but you have my word I won't say a thing to anyone," Catherine said seriously.

"I'm not sure if I've unloaded a burden or a relief on you. I would want to know if it was me in your shoes, but I'd hate to have something so close I could touch it and so forbidden I wouldn't dare," Elizabeth said.

"Who says I want to touch anything?" Catherine tilted her chin just a notch.

CHAPTER TEN

Catherine dressed with care in a dark green silk dress trimmed with velveteen ribbon. The high turnover collar and narrow cuffs were mint green satin and matched the covered buttons set down the left side of the tunic effect over the narrow skirted dress.

Bridget wore a tailored skirt in navy blue that stopped mid calf styled with a cross belt in front. She'd topped it with a pale blue silk blouse with a deep squared collar of Chantilly lace. Alice would rather wear her overalls and sketch the preacher with his bulging eyes and hallow cheeks, but she'd learned early in life that Momma did not condone such things in church. So she'd chosen a blue plaid skirt with a simple middy blouse and navy silk tie. They wore matching smart toque hats of satin finished straw braid trimmed with off white satin hand bands.

The morning was drab with solid gray skies threatening to drop rain at any moment. Bridget carried two platters of ham to the car. Alice toted a chocolate cake and a peach cobbler and Catherine brought up the rear with a basket of freshly sliced yeast bread. They would be well represented that day at the church social after services and looked forward to a Sunday dinner they didn't have to serve. Catherine drove and wished she'd remembered their slickers, or at least an umbrella. They'd look like three drowned rats if they had to run from the car to the church in a downpour. At least those thoughts kept her mind off Quincy but not for long. By the time they were safe and dry inside the church the thoughts had begun to wander again.

Alice nodded to a couple of people and headed straight for their normal pew. Bridget smiled at Annabel on the way. Catherine followed without seeing anyone. They'd sat in the same place since the first Sunday the church opened its doors; third from the back on the left side of the center aisle.

The church had been built at the same time Patrick O'Shea put up the Black Swan. Four stained glass windows on each side of the sanctuary let in filtered light. Two rows

170

of pews with a center aisle and no room at the sides to get in and out. Children were taught at an early age they'd best go at home or take advantage of the two holed outhouse down the path behind the church because it was rude to crawl across people once they were seated. The raised pulpit was behind a waist high petition with just enough room at the top for candles which were lit that gray morning to bring in a little warmth and light.

The pastor, a gaunt looking fellow with a receding hair line and brown eyes, had lost his wife to the flu about the same time Patrick died. He'd been eyeing Catherine as a replacement as soon as the mourning period was over and smiled brightly when he saw her enter the church with her sisters. Six more months and he'd be moving her out of that hotel and into the parsonage. Or else he'd be moving into the spacious hotel with her. He looked forward to home cooked meals and someone to do the laundry and Catherine was almighty easy on the eyes. Of course, he'd have a bit of a job with her free thinking, but he could tame that in a hurry. After all, it was a man's job to keep his wife under control. The Bible supported him with the verses about women submitting to their husbands.

She felt Quincy's presence long before she actually saw him. Her neck began to itch and her heart skipped a half-beat; her hands were clammy and she twisted her hanky into a knot. When he sat down behind her she got a whiff of the lotion he splashed on his face after he shaved and for the first time in her life felt like she might have the vapors right there in the church in front of Pastor Dan, the whole congregation and even God.

Elizabeth touched her on the shoulder. "Good morning."

She didn't actually jump. It was more of a quiver that ran through her body. "Good morning. You startled me."

Quincy nodded. "Miss O'Shea?"

"Mr. Massey." Catherine held her head high and looked at the man in the last pew right behind Quincy. She didn't dare look right at him or her eyes would go all soft. If Elizabeth could see something there, then she wouldn't be able to hide it from others.

Pastor Dan took his place, cleared his throat loudly and smiled out across the full church. "If you will turn your hymn books to page five, we can all sing together."

Five. Now why did he have to choose that number? Does Quincy know that he kissed me five times that night on the river bank? Does he ever think of those kisses?

172

With his deep tone she'd expected him to sing beautifully and was surprised to hear a barely passable voice behind her that had trouble staying on key and in tune. Elizabeth actually did a much better job with her lovely soprano voice. Catherine wondered if she'd ever sung on the stage.

The sermon that morning was about going on after defeat. Pastor Dan talked about the losses they'd had in the community and how they should put that behind them and go on with their lives, doing good for God.

Catherine listened with half an ear, and even that was difficult. Quincy was three feet behind her. It was like going to the candy store with a whole quarter. Having the money in her hand to buy anything she wanted in the store and being told she wasn't to spend one cent. She could look at the candy but she couldn't have a single peppermint stick. No touching. No partaking. Barely looking.

Silently she cursed Elizabeth for telling her. It would have been easier just thinking he was married than sitting in hell right in the middle of the church.

"We'll close in a word of prayer," Pastor Dan said.

Catherine bowed her head and jerked her thoughts back to reality.

"Amen," he said after several minutes of praising God for everything under the sun up to and including the new people in his congregation. "And now, as you all know we are having a pot luck lunch to break in our brand new fellowship room. It is a place where we can have meetings, funeral dinners and wedding receptions and we are very proud of it. Please join us for fellowship and food. Everyone is welcome."

Women set about getting food dishes uncovered and on the tables in some kind of organized method. Meats and vegetables on one long table. Desserts on another. Plates in the proper place so the lines could move along rapidly. Little girls set the brand new eight foot tables by throwing a table cloth on first and then placing napkins and flatware in front of every chair.

Elizabeth chose to work beside Catherine. "I made chocolate pies this week. Quincy said they were almost as good as the ones at the Black Swan. I think he just said that so I'd try again. Did you know chocolate is his favorite pie? He likes peach cobbler but it can't hold a light to chocolate. And ham? That man could eat his weight in ham, I do believe. If I served it every night he'd be happy as a little piglet in a fresh spring mud hole."

"Hmmmm," Catherine filed that information away . . . just in case.

"Would you look at this gorgeous carrot cake? Did you make it? And is that seven minute frosting on the top? Someone surely put in a lot of time on this," Elizabeth prattled on.

Alice piped up on the other side of Catherine. "Mabel made that. She makes all the wedding cakes around here. Lovely things. She made Bridget's. Come to think of it, I don't think I want her to make mine."

"Oh, are you getting married?" Elizabeth asked.

Alice winked. "One never knows what might happen, do they?"

Catherine stopped dead, a cake knife in her hands, and cocked her head to one side. "Is there something you haven't told me?" She asked Alice.

"No. Is there something you haven't told me?" She turned the tables on Catherine.

"Oh, stop it. Cut those pies. The men and boys will be in here ready to eat in a few minutes. Pastor Dan . . . Great God, are you seeing him on the sly?" Catherine cut her eyes toward Alice.

Alice snarled her nose. "God is great but I expect you'd best watch out if lightning starts flashing around, using his name in vain right here in the church and on Sunday. But to answer your question, I wouldn't have a chance with Pastor Dan even if I was interested. He's got his next wife picked out and it's you." She pointed her finger at Catherine.

Elizabeth stopped cutting the carrot cake into wedges. "Oh, really?"

"No, not really. God almighty, I'm not cut out to be a preacher's wife," Catherine said.

"Talking like that, I tend to agree with you," Alice giggled.

"Watch out. He might sneak up on your blind side," Elizabeth whispered.

Mabel brought another cake to the table. "What? Whose blind side?"

"Pastor Dan," Alice said.

Catherine was waving the knife and flashing drop dead looks at her sister behind Mabel's back.

"What about that poor, poor soul? He loved his wife so much. Who's trying to sneak up on his blind side?" Mabel asked.

"No one," Catherine said.

Alice lowered her voice to a high whisper. "It's him doing the sneaking. Did you know that he's been asking about Clarissa Miles? That sweet lady lost her husband in that saw mill accident a few months ago. Don't you think they'd make a lovely couple?"

"Oh, yes, well, I must get on back to my post. I'm serving vegetables," Mabel said.

"You owe me," Alice said.

Elizabeth snickered behind her hand. She'd always wanted a sister. Maybe she'd adopt the whole trio of O'Shea's. "Whatever it's going to cost Catherine, I'll help pay the price just for the fun of seeing what happens this afternoon."

"I want tomorrow off. I want to sketch during daylight hours instead of working in the kitchen. You up for a stint of serving and cooking?" Alice said.

"That's rude," Catherine said.

"No, it's not. I'll be there at eight o'clock and Alice, remind me that if I'm ever in trouble to call on you. Dang, you are good," Elizabeth said.

"Yes, I am. I'm glad someone sees my talents."

Pastor Dan led the men and boys in from the lawn where they'd been discussing the effects the war's end would have on the saw mill and consequently their whole town. He gave a short grace and dinner began, everyone helping themselves to mountains of food.

Elizabeth and Quincy insisted the O'Shea's share their table. Pastor Dan joined them along with Mabel, Henry and

Clarissa. Catherine watched Clarissa work her wiles on Pastor Dan, who bless his heart, didn't know he was about to get himself tangled up in Cupid's sticky web.

"So did the young men staying at the Black Swan last week find work around here?" Quincy asked.

"Oh, no, they went on to Marion to see if the railroad was hiring. But I wouldn't be surprised if Baxter comes back before long. He was quite taken with Catherine. Asked her to take a walk with him but she said she didn't step out with customers," Alice said.

Catherine could have strangled her. There was plenty of room in the hole where they'd put Ralph. She would dig the hole by herself this time and toss in the shovel with Alice's cold, dead body. It would be a good thing for her to be absent from the hotel the next day. It could be the very thing that saved her life.

Quincy's heart weighed a ton. He should have thought about the possibility of other men being interested in the beautiful Catherine. He was in a position where he couldn't say a word for weeks and during that time he could easily lose any hope of ever being in a position to kiss her again.

Elizabeth turned her innocent blue eyed stare to Quincy. "Was that the good looking dark haired man we met in the lobby that first night I arrived?"

"That would be the one," Alice answered for him.

Catherine promptly kicked her under the table.

"Well, let's hope he finds a wonderful job and comes courtin'. Wouldn't that be nice?" Elizabeth acted the part of big eyed wonder as if she didn't know one thing and was really married to Quincy.

Pastor Dan cleared his throat. "One should be very careful, Catherine. We'll see lots of drifters in the next few months with the war over and men hunting work. There could be some real scalawags amongst them. I'm not so sure you ladies should be staying at the hotel without benefit of a man's presence."

"We can manage. Anything a man can do, Catherine can do. We'll be just fine," Bridget said.

"Should you ever feel threatened, you just send word to me. I'll be glad to occupy one of the hotel rooms for you," Pastor Dan offered.

Good God, Alice was right.

Elizabeth tapped Catherine's thigh under the table and turned her brilliance toward the preacher. "What a wonderful gesture?

Clarissa, do you ever feel frightened living all alone since your husband was taken so abruptly?"

"Oh, yes, sometimes it's a difficult thing just to fall asleep. My dear Harry left for work right after breakfast and the next day we were burying him. It takes a long time to get over such a thing, doesn't it, Pastor Dan? Sometimes at night I am frightened. It's always nice to have a good, strong man around."

Pastor Dan patted her hand and really saw her for the first time. Long brown hair done up in a tidy bun on top of her head. Dress buttoned up to her neck where a circle of lace formed a lovely collar. Skirt still at the top of her ankle where it should be. This new style of skirts worn half way up to the knee just gave way to lustful ideas. He was glad some women were still modest. Why hadn't he seen her before?

Taming Catherine would be the same as taming a wild mountain lion. It would give a man a certain power. But Pastor Dan wasn't any man; he was a man of God. And he should be looking for a woman who wouldn't disgrace his position. With a faint sigh, he turned his attention back to Clarissa. Sometimes it was a real trial to do the right.

■ ■ ■ ■

Quincy didn't taste a bite of his dinner. He
might as well have been chewing on saw
dust held together with wood glue. Catherine was so close he could reach out and
touch her but Elizabeth was between them.
For the next six weeks that would be the
situation and there was nothing he could
do.

He'd uncovered nothing at the mill but it
had only been two weeks. Elizabeth had
been more prosperous in her endeavors the
past week. She'd picked up gossip at two
afternoon visits that could be a lead. The
next morning he'd approach the six men
who could be the core for the unrest. Hopefully the situation could be resolved much
quicker than the original plan.

He and Elizabeth drove home in the
middle of the afternoon. He opened the
door and allowed her to enter before him
just like a dutiful husband. The whole house
was smaller than the bedroom he'd had as a
child growing up in Little Rock. The front
door opened right into the living room. Elizabeth had set a shoe tree on the left wall so
he'd have a place to hang his hat and sit to
put on his boots in the morning. A small

settee, a rocking chair, an overstuffed blue velvet easy chair for him, a few tables with doilies and lamps and the room was full. The Oldham's had papered not long before they'd evacuated so it was clean if ugly.

The kitchen was straight ahead and two doors opened off the hallway into bedrooms papered in the same pink and white flowers with vines that threatened to jump off the walls and strangle Quincy. He had the bedroom to the right; Elizabeth's was on the left.

Elizabeth sank down in the rocking chair and kicked her shoes off, wigging her toes inside her stockings. "That went well. Alice told us that Preacher Dan was eyeing Catherine for the next preacher's wife. So we told Mabel that Preacher Dan had his heart set on Clarissa. That's all it took. She had them hooked up tight by the end of the day. My experiment worked, Quincy. Tomorrow I'm going to the Black Swan to work in Alice's place so she can have a day off. I'm going to use the afternoon between meals to visit Mabel. I think I can steer her toward helping us take care of this job. Well-placed gossip sometimes nets the best information. I'm ready to go home. I really do not like this place."

"You'd never know it," he grumbled.

"What's got a burr in your hind end?" She asked.

"Nothing. I'm taking a nap."

"It's Alice, isn't it? You've fallen for her."

"It most certainly is not."

"Catherine?" She tossed out.

He was silent.

"It is Catherine. Now isn't that a fine fedder. You didn't tell me the whole story about the Black Swan experience did you? You've gone and fallen for an Irish lass who thinks you are married and there's nothing you can do about it. Well, darlin' cousin, let's get this job sewed up. I'm ready to go home and plan a wedding and evidently you need to plan a courtin'."

"I couldn't court her now if I wanted to. This town is so small that everyone knows I'm married. Catherine wouldn't marry a divorced man and I wouldn't ask her to do so and the truth would destroy our work anyway. It's a pickle isn't it?"

"One never knows about tomorrow. I just know if I have to sleep in this room much longer those vines are going to come alive and attack me like a Python."

Quincy chuckled. "You too? I swear they really do grow every night. Maybe they're like the kudzu over in the deep south. That stuff grows a foot a day."

She got up from the rocker and hugged him. "We'll get through it. I promise."

"I don't see how that's possible," he said.

Catherine changed from her Sunday best into a pair of overalls. They'd offer supper that night to any wayfarers who might wander into the hotel but she didn't expect many takers. She picked up the romance book she'd ordered the month before: *Maid of the Whispering Hills* by Vingie E. Roe, a four hundred page novel about a woman who had three men in love with her.

"How on earth did she manage that? I couldn't even function with the possibility of one man being remotely interested," she mumbled as she turned the first page of the green cloth covered book.

"Were you talking to me?" Bridget asked.

"No, I'm just muttering to myself. Can you imagine having three men in love with you?"

Bridget shuddered hard enough to shake her hair loose from its pins. "I wouldn't want to imagine such a nightmare. Ralph said he loved me and look what that brought on. I sure wouldn't want to deal with three devils."

"You'll get over it and find someone who appreciates you for who and what you are,"

Catherine said.

"No thank you. Me and Ella are going to do just fine by ourselves," Bridget said. "I'm sorry about Quincy, Catherine. I know you kind of had a liking for him. It showed in your eyes. I think he would've liked you, too, if he hadn't already been married."

"Thanks," Catherine propped pillows at the head of her four poster bed and used them to support her back as she read. If she took a deep breath, she could still smell Quincy's lotion. If she shut her eyes she could see the misery in his eyes.

She popped her eyes wide open and made herself read. She didn't need to dwell on something she couldn't have.

CHAPTER ELEVEN

What sun filtered through the tall pine trees was warm on Catherine's face as she leaned back against the stump and watched the fishing bobble dance on the waves of the river. She fully understood her father's words that day and didn't care if she caught a single fish. She'd come to the river to think; fishing was secondary.

A postcard arrived in the mail the day before from Marion, Louisiana. The front pictured a soldier with his arm around a red haired woman dressed in white. On the back was a brief note from Baxter saying they'd found jobs in the area and he'd be back to ask her to go on that walk in five months. Until then she was to keep him in her heart.

"How can I keep Baxter in my heart when every nook and cranny is filled with someone else?" She muttered.

Her eyes focused on the bobble without

seeing it. She had to get past this thing with Quincy and move on with her life. Perhaps Baxter would be a good choice. He was hard working and apparently taken with her. She could give him a chance at least, get to know him and figure out whether he was another Ralph.

Or Preacher Dan. Clarissa was smiling a lot more these past two weeks and Mabel had it out over the hot gossip lines that there would no doubt be a lady in the parsonage before long. But Catherine wasn't totally unaware of the looks he kept throwing toward her in church.

That thought brought her to the fact that Quincy and Elizabeth weren't in church that morning. As a matter of fact she hadn't seen Elizabeth since Wednesday when she'd come by the hotel and wound up helping serve lunch. She hoped her new found friend wasn't ill. Maybe on her way home she'd better run by the Oldham place and make sure Elizabeth was all right.

Of course that brought her right back to Quincy. When he spoke so close to her side that she could feel the warmth of his breath on her neck, she jumped. At first she figured it was just another figment of her imagination but a quick look found him sitting close enough that he was leaning on the same stump.

He wore the same old overalls and flannel shirt he'd had on the night the storm stranded them in the car. He smelled heavenly and from the grooves in his hair, he'd combed it hurriedly with his fingers.

"Catchin' anything?" He asked.

"Not yet. What are you doing here? Where's your fishin' pole?"

"I don't have one. Didn't think about borrowing one from the tool shed. Went by the hotel and saw the car gone and just took a chance you'd be down here," he said.

"Is something wrong with Elizabeth?"

"No, not really. She caught the noon train to Little Rock this morning. That's why we weren't in church. She was homesick so I sent her home for a week."

"How'd you get here?"

"I borrowed Major's horse and rode," he said.

"There'll be talk if anyone sees you," she said.

He reached across the space and cupped her chin with his hand, turning her face so he could look into her eyes. "You know, don't you?"

She jerked away. At least she didn't whimper like a puppy wanting to have his belly

188

rubbed, but she dang sure felt like it. "Know what?"

"Either she told you or you figured it out on your own. I swear you are clairvoyant," Quincy said.

"Are you daft? What are you talking about?"

"Elizabeth and I are not married. She's my cousin and this is nothing more than a job," he blurted out.

"Oh, that."

"Why didn't you tell me you knew? Lord, it's been a horrible long month and . . ."

"So I know. What now?" She asked.

"Well, for starters, there is going to be a big layoff tomorrow at the mill. I'm at the top of the list and I'll be packing my belongings and going on back to Little Rock. Most likely by the end of the week. I'll stay around a few days and hunt for other work but it won't be forth coming. Those are my orders," he said.

"And?"

"I'm attracted to you and I think you feel the same. But things are very complicated right now. Everyone thinks I'm married. What do you think we should do?"

The hardest word Catherine ever said had trouble leaving her lips. "Wait."

"I suppose that's the best thing."

"If it's meant to be, it will. If not, then it was just an attraction between two lonely people," she said.

He sighed.

"I really didn't like you," she said.

"I really didn't like you. You are pig headed and conniving. You knew Ralph wasn't buried in that garden and you let me spend a whole day hunting for him. I still bet you know where he is and won't tell."

"That would fix this problem in a hurry, now wouldn't it? I'd be in jail and you'd be off on another job with the lovely Elizabeth or some other woman who isn't even your relative. I couldn't be married to a man like that Quincy. I'd never be comfortable with you taking off with some other lady even if it was a job," she said.

"I didn't propose."

She blushed. "You know what I mean. Don't pick a fight just because things didn't go your way. I think you were attracted to me in the beginning because it was safe. You couldn't act on it because it was a conflict of interest with your job. Then it was safe because you were married. Now it's not safe and you're running back to Little Rock."

"If that's the case, it won't ever be safe because I always close my cases and Ralph's is still open. If you've got anything to do with his disappearance you'd better 'fess up now," he said.

Great Scot, he hadn't planned on riding out there to fight with her. Far from it and yet that's exactly what they were doing. He'd been mooning after the wrong woman. Because he couldn't have her he'd set her up on a pedestal and admired her from afar. The closer he got the more her true colors popped out and he didn't like them one bit.

"You are the big mean detective. You find him, darlin', if you've a mind to go lookin' anywhere else on my property. Come to think of it, you never did dig up the root cellar or the basement."

"Good God, you've got a basement?" He asked.

"Yes to both. God is good and yes, we have a basement but you didn't ask," she smarted off.

"A basement in this kind of place where there's bogs and . . . how do you keep it dry?"

"Papa knew what to do. I never asked and it doesn't fill up with water so there," she said.

"Dirt floor?"

"Of course. It's not a place for tea parties. There's a furnace down there we keep fueled in the winter and the generator for our refrigerator. Momma's washing machine even though these days we send the laundry out. You can move it all around if you've a mind to dig again. You know where the shovels are."

He moaned.

"Is Ralph buried in the basement?"

"No, he is not," she said.

"I'm going to believe you, but this would always be between us wouldn't it?"

"Just like your marriage. Even though it wasn't true, my sisters and everyone in town thinks it is."

They sat in silence for several minutes.

"Guess I'd best get on back," he said.

"Have a good trip and give my best to Elizabeth. Tell her to write. I liked her a lot," Catherine said around a lump in her throat.

"Know why she left early? Because she hates good-byes."

Catherine turned to look at him, to freeze his face into her heart forever. "So do I."

He turned at the same time and leaned forward. The kiss rivaled all of the ones they'd shared in the car.

He stood up, brushed the dirt from the seat of his overalls, mounted the horse he had tied to the back of her Ford and rode away. "Then we won't say good-bye, Catherine O'Shea."

Two days later on a Tuesday morning Alice brought in the mail. There was a letter accompanying the formal divorce decree from the judge in El Dorado. He wrote that it was with sadness of heart that he granted the divorce but several things had come to light and he was of the opinion that if a man deserted his wife then she had the right to divorce him. It was a great moment in the Black Swan and Bridget cried as she hugged her sisters.

The second letter was from Sophia Contiello, Ralph's mother. It was to inform Bridget that they would not be responsible for any of her financial needs. It went on to say that she was never to darken their doorstep again and that they held her personally responsible for their son's death. Had she stayed home and obeyed him like a wife should then he wouldn't have been in Huttig that night he went missing.

Bridget read it aloud, put it back in the envelope and dried her tears. "I will not cry again, ever. It's over and I'm Bridget O'Shea. That's who I'll be until the day I die."

"Whew, don't be so fast to declare such a

thing," Catherine said.

"If that's the way she feels then it's her right," Alice argued. "And here is another post card from Baxter to Catherine."

Catherine snatched it just as Alice turned it over to see what he'd written. All it said was *four months and counting.* The picture on the front was a vase with a dozen roses in it.

"And one for me," Alice held up an envelope. "Can you believe that? It's from Elizabeth. Shall I read it aloud?"

Catherine nodded.

"That would be nice." Bridget put the divorce paper in a special box where they kept the deed to the land the hotel was built on and Momma and Papa's wills.

"Okay, here goes:

Dear Alice, Catherine and Bridget,

I feel I owe you ladies an apology for not having said good-bye and for leaving so quickly. I did enjoy our days in your hotel and your friendship.

Before I married Quincy I had a short marriage to another man who was killed in the war. I got a telegram saying he had died in action and a letter from his captain telling me and his family that he was an honorable man. Last Sunday I received a telegram. My first husband had not died. He was captured and spent the rest of the time in a prisoner of war camp over there somewhere. It took the government these past five months to get him back to Little Rock.

What a predicament? I caught the next train out of Huttig and met with my lawyers and a judge, as well as saw my husband again. I'd forgotten how much I did love him. Under the strange circumstances, it has been decided I must be married to my first husband and the marriage to Quincy will be annulled.

We have decided to move away from all the gossip that would surround us and live in Memphis, Tennessee where he has a good job.

My best to all of you.

Elizabeth

Catherine bit the inside of her lip to keep from giggling. What a story. Only Elizabeth could have come up with such a lie. She really should write it up in the form of a script and sell it to the movie industry.

"How sad," Bridget said.

"Sad. It's the biggest crock I've ever heard. She never was married to Quincy and this is just a story we're supposed to tell so it looks good," Alice said.

"What makes you think that?" Catherine asked.

"Because it could never happen. What would you do if Ira came walking in the door? Toss Baxter out with the dishwater? Tell Pastor Dan to quit looking at you with those big old soulful eyes? The government don't send those telegrams out saying a soldier is dead unless he's dead," Alice protested.

"Mistakes happen," Catherine said.

"God, I hope not," Alice said.

"You want Ira to be dead? You want me to encourage the preacher or Baxter?" Catherine asked.

Alice threw up her hands in an angry gesture. To explain would cause a major fight amongst them. "No, I don't want Ira to be dead. Yes, I want you to encourage someone."

"Why?" Catherine asked.

"It doesn't matter. I'm going out for a walk."

She made it to the lobby and found Mabel coming in the front door.

"Good afternoon. I was wondering if you girls had an extra pie in the kitchen. I just got word that Annabel is ill and they're bringing the afternoon bridge club to my house. I'd like to buy a pie for refreshments if there's an extra one," Mabel said.

Catherine opened the door into the lobby when she heard voices.

"Mabel needs a pie for her bridge club this afternoon. You can take care of it. And tell her all about poor old Quincy while you're at it. It's not a secret, you know." Alice talked as she headed out into the warm sunshine.

"Whatever is the matter with her? She looks mad enough to spit," Mabel said.

"Oh, who knows what Alice is ever thinking," Catherine said.

Mabel followed her into the kitchen. Catherine picked up a chocolate pie and Mabel nodded.

"Shall I put it on your tab? You can pick up the charge when you and Henry come in for your Friday night outing."

"Yes, yes, that would be nice. What was Alice talking about poor Quincy? Has Elizabeth's mother died?" Mabel asked.

"No but Elizabeth's first husband didn't either." Catherine told her the whole fabricated story which Mabel ate up faster than she would the pie. Her bridge club would be in hog heaven that afternoon with so much ridiculous gossip to feed on.

"That poor soul, and he was so much in

love with Elizabeth. Why it just poured out of his heart every time he looked at her. I shall remember him in my prayers but I doubt he ever finds another woman to take her place. Sometimes there's only one love for a man and I'm afraid Elizabeth was his. I'm never wrong about matters of the heart, you know." She said it with a sniff and slight tilt to her hawkish nose.

"Maybe he'll just give his heart to his job," Catherine offered.

"Oh, dear, didn't you hear? He was laid off yesterday and left last night on the train back to Little Rock. First he loses his detective job because of . . . well . . ." she stammered and blushed. "Because he couldn't find Bridget's husband. Then he loses his wife and his job at the mill. I just feel so sorry for him. Oh, I just remembered something else I wanted to talk to you about. I heard that there was a letter from the law firm or the courthouse or some such thing that came to Bridget. Why would she be getting a letter from them?"

"Didn't you know? She filed for divorce from Ralph. He deserted her and she doesn't want to be married to him so the judge granted it," Catherine said. Might as well get the whole ball of wax out and let Mabel really hold court that afternoon.

"Oh, my, oh my," Mabel set the pie down on a table and clutched the front of her dress like her heart was fixing to stop beating. "Whatever will happen now? Our little town with a divorced woman. We'll be a disgrace. I'm sure it will hurt your business."

"We'll manage," Catherine said.

"But . . ."

Catherine decided to let a few more cats out of the bag. "She just wanted out of the marriage. She didn't want to bring up her child in such a bad atmosphere."

"Child?" Mabel blanched.

"Yes, she's taken her maiden name back because she didn't want her baby to be a Contiello. It will be born an O'Shea since that's her name."

Mabel grabbed for the back of a chair. "When is this event due to happen?"

"Sometime in September," Catherine said. "She's been knitting pink blankets. I told her she'd best have a few blue things. What do you think?"

"I think I'd better get this pie on home and get ready for the club. I just can't imagine what your mother would say if she were alive." Mabel headed for the door.

"Oh, she'd be tickled. Bridget says she's naming the baby Ella."

Catherine waited until Mabel was across the hotel lawn and in her house before she broke into hysterical laughter that brought on a case of hiccups. Bridget came out into the lobby because she thought Catherine and Alice were arguing and one of them was crying. Between bouts of giggles Catherine told her what she'd just done.

Bridget patted her stomach. "Good, now I can stop wearing those tight skirts and start wearing smocks. Ella, did you hear that? We've gone public with you."

Chapter Twelve

Catherine walked out of the bank in El Dorado in a daze. She'd known the hotel had done a good business through her growing up years but she'd had no idea she and her sisters were so comfortable financially. She checked her watch to find she had an hour before time to board the train back to Huttig and for a moment stood outside the bank in bewilderment. She could hardly wait to get home to the Black Swan, but excitement couldn't make the train leave early.

Finally she headed toward the station, taking time to looking in the store windows on the way. She stepped inside a clothing store and spent a few minutes at the counter holding the little girl dresses and bloomers. Touching the clothing made it real for the first time that she was actually going to be an aunt. Boy or girl, there would be a child in the hotel again.

Lord, please let it be a girl. Not a one of us

would have a single notion about raising a boy child, she prayed.

She picked up a pink cotton sunbonnet. A cute little thing with a button on the back. No fullness to leave wrinkles in little Ella's neck when she was lying down. Or to give Bridget grief when she was ironing it, either. She almost laid it back down, it was so definitely a girl item, but she couldn't. It called out to her and even though Bridget would fuss at her for spending so much on something they could make from calico scraps, she'd be proud of it at the same time.

"This all for you today?" The clerk asked.

"Yes, ma'am."

"That will be twenty–nine cents," she said. "Do I know you? You look so familiar."

"I don't think so," Catherine answered.

"That's right. You just look somewhat like a customer who used to come in fairly often. She had red hair but it wasn't nearly as dark as yours and green eyes but they were lighter. She was married to the Contiello man who went missing several months ago. I felt sorry for her. That man was a bully his whole life. The reason he didn't find a wife from here and had to go to another town was because we all kept our distance from him."

"Imagine that? Was he good looking?"

Catherine asked.

"Very much so. And rich. And his family had connections. But honey, even that don't hold water if your husband is mean as a snake. Anyway, you remind me of his wife."

"She's my sister," Catherine finally admitted.

"I heard she'd gone back to her family. Tell her she did the smart thing and tell her Inez says hello. She'll remember me. We talked often." She handed Catherine the bonnet in brown paper tied with twine.

"I'll be glad to give her your greetings. Good-day, now," Catherine said.

She peeked in each window as she made her way back to the rail station. She'd ridden the train the previous evening and spent the night in a nice hotel. At breakfast in the hotel a new type of sugar dispensers were on the tables. She found them sitting in a display in one of the windows, went inside and ordered a dozen to be shipped to the Black Swan. The bad thing about sugar bowls was that the lids got broken and couldn't be replaced. The new, innovative sugar containers had a metal screw on lid with a hole in the top to literally pour the sugar into the tea or on the oatmeal.

She stopped in a general merchandise store and bought a package of Old Maid cards for Alice. She did love that silly game and giggled over the crazy names on them: Hans Dutch, Susie Sweet, Phelim O'Pfat and Golfer McCaddie.

When she checked her watch again, she was amazed to find she'd whiled away too much time and had to hurry to the train station. The conductor was making a final call when she stepped inside and found a place to sit. It wasn't until she'd settled into the wooden seat and caught her breath that she looked up to see who was sitting across from her.

Her heart stopped and she forgot to breathe. Finally, she gasped.

"Hello, Catherine," Quincy said.

"What are you doing here?" She asked bluntly.

"I'm on my way to the coast for a little relaxation. And you?"

"Business trip for the hotel."

"Are your sisters well?"

"Oh, yes, they're fine. Elizabeth?"

"In the last planning stages of her wedding. I'll get home in time to be a part of it."

They looked out the window at the tall pines whizzing past. Fate had brought them together; nothing else could have put them on the same train, in the same seating area at the same time. It was pure chance and would never happen again.

They had time to talk alone but Huttig was the next stop and wasn't that far away. Suddenly Catherine was tongue tied and couldn't think of anything else to say. If she opened her mouth, she'd pour out her soul and make a complete fool of herself. If she kept it shut, she'd think of hundreds of things she could have said but it would be too late.

Quincy had to make a move even if it netted him nothing. He could say what was in his heart or wonder the rest of his life whether things might have been different if he'd swallowed his pride and simply asked her.

"Cath . . ."

"Quin . . ."

He smiled. "You first."

"No, you started first so what were you going to say?"

"Have you ever been to the coast?"

"No, when Momma and Papa got into the hotel business it was a seven day job. We've all been to El Dorado with them at different times and once, after we got the Ford, Papa drove us to Marion. Other than that, it's been Huttig."

"Want to go? My family owns a home

right on the sand in Avalon Beach, Florida."

She looked deeply into his dark brown eyes. "Are you asking me?"

"That I am. I've got two weeks. It's a big house and well secluded, but if anyone asked, you could be my cousin."

Her breath caught again but she swallowed the gasp. She couldn't leave the hotel for two weeks. Bridget and Alice would be livid if she even suggested such a thing.

"Tell you what," he said. "I'll get off in Huttig and spend the night at the Commercial. Be at the station tomorrow at ten o'clock if you want to go. If not, simply stay at home."

"Fair enough," she said. There was no way she could be there even his asking sent her imagination and emotions into a whirlwind.

"Oh, and Catherine, I will be a gentleman."

"Thank you," she said. Did that mean she had to be a lady?

"And I promise not to mention Ralph."

"It wouldn't do you any good."

Quincy ate at the Commercial that night even though he would have much rather found Major and taken him to dinner at the Black Swan. He opened his suitcase and removed a book. It had been at least three years since he'd had time to read anything except the morning newspapers. His contributions to the war effort took all his time for a large portion of the three years; then there was the Contiello case and the routing out of dissidents at the saw mill. He'd spent three days at home with his parents but good cooking didn't hold his attention long. He was restless and he'd been promised two weeks. That's when he remembered the shore and the house there. It must have been an omen because if he'd gone north to the cabin in the mountains he would have never crossed paths with Catherine.

When he'd boarded the train bound for the seashore in Florida he'd done it with thoughts of ridding his mind of a certain red haired lady who kept invading every minute of his time. Who would have thought she'd be on the same train? Suddenly, a million questions bombarded him. What on earth would they talk about for two whole weeks? All they'd done up to then was argue and kiss. Now the kisses, they could set his body ablaze and fry his brain, but he'd just promised to be a gentleman. What could he be thinking, asking her to accompany him? The right thing for him to do was pack his bags and take the midnight train anywhere it was going. She wouldn't be there tomorrow morning anyway. He'd just set himself up for a big disappointment.

Alice had insisted the afternoon before that Catherine take the Ford to the station. If they needed it, they could easily get Henry to drive them down to retrieve it. Catherine was glad when she saw it still sitting in the place where she'd parked it; that meant everything was fine at home. She opened the door and slid her suitcase over into the passenger's seat. Her hat brim caught the top of the frame when she bent to get in so she had to reposition it. That's when she saw Quincy walking toward the Commercial Hotel. She was about to give him a ride but decided against it. The decision in front of her would be difficult enough without sitting beside him in the very car where they'd shared all those wonderful kisses.

Pastor Dan was sitting on the porch when Catherine drove into the yard. He had a cup of coffee and a platter of cookies beside him and was fanning his face with his straw hat. He wore his Sunday suit and his shoes were polished to a shine.

She retrieved her suitcase and carried it to the porch. Of all the people in the world she wanted to see right then he was at the very bottom of the list. She had to be kind because God had answered her prayers that night when they'd taken care of things with Ralph and not gotten caught. She'd begged that no one catch them digging that hole or dragging three shovels back to the tool shed. Now here sat a man of God so she felt duty bound to be nice but it came at great sacrifice.

"Good afternoon. How are you?" She asked.

"I'm fit as a fiddle. Yes it is a bit warm. Sticky with the recent rain and now this blistering heat. We're in for a summer, we are. I understand you've been on a trip to El Dorado. Did everything go well?"

"Everything went just fine. I bought the new baby a bonnet and Alice a deck of Old Maid cards," she said.

"Do you think that is prudent? Buying for a child that will come into this world as a . . ." he fumbled around the offensive word.

"A bastard? I don't think so. It will come into this world as a loved child in the O'Shea family. We'll fight unto the death if anyone calls it that abominable name."

"It does seem a bit premature to buy gifts for an unborn child when you don't know if it's a girl or boy," he protested. This wasn't going nearly as well as he'd hoped.

"Perhaps, but Bridget wants a girl. With all she's been through, I think God owes her that," Catherine said. She knew she was snappish and at that moment didn't care that she was talking to the preacher.

Preacher Dan shook his finger at her. "God does not owe Bridget one thing. That's not the way it works, Catherine. And while we're discussing your trip, do you think it's wise to bring cards into your home?"

"What's the matter with a silly card game?" She asked.

"It's time wasted. You could spend that time getting to know your Lord and Savior better through his word," he said. Might as well make her understand what her position would be as his wife.

"Time is not wasted when it's spent with family and having a good time," she protested. "I'm going inside. I have to talk to my sisters. If you'll pardon me, please."

She started into the house. In one swift motion he was on his feet and had reached out and grabbed her arm.

"I'm sorry to have offended you but I came here for a purpose. I'm thinking on asking Clarissa to be my bride and . . ."

She removed his hand, dropping it like it was a dead bird or a piece of garbage.

"Congratulations to you both." She opened the screen door.

"Before I do, I want to know if there's a chance for us, Catherine. I've had my eye on you for a long while now and I do believe we could be a good couple. I would not be averse to living here at the hotel with you so you wouldn't have to give up your home. However, we would have to discuss where Bridget would live."

"I think you'd better ask Clarissa. My sister isn't going anywhere. I'm not in love with you, Pastor Dan," she gritted between clenched teeth.

He tilted his bony chin up and glared at her. "Catherine O'Shea, you need a firm hand to keep you in line. All of you O'Shea women are far too wild. There was hope for Bridget when she was married to Ralph but I'm afraid you are turning down the best offer you will ever get in Huttig."

"This time you get a warning — if you ever mention my sister like that again, I will make you wish you had never survived birth." She went inside the house and left him on the porch with his hat in his hand.

She found her sisters in the living room. Bridget had her feet propped on a footstool watching Alice put the finishing touches on a painting she'd been working on for weeks.

"Hey, what did you find out? Are we going belly up if the saw mill lays off a bunch more men?" Alice asked.

"Daddy left us well off, ladies. He and Momma saved a lot of money. We are not rich but we will manage very well. I brought the report in my suitcase so you can see the actual figures," Catherine said.

Alice laid her brush down. "Then why the long face. Hey, there's another post card from Baxter. I read it. He says he's coming around in two weeks just in case you've forgotten what he looks like. And it's got the cutest little bunny on the front of it."

Catherine told them everything the preacher had said.

"Oh, ignore him. We know what we're doing and it don't matter what he thinks," Bridget said.

"Poor Clarissa doesn't know what she's in for. Shall we tell her?" Alice asked.

"No, we will not," Bridget said. "I think she's got more backbone than she lets be seen. He might be biting off more than he can chew."

"I hope to hell he is," Catherine said.

"Now, that's out in the open and you shouldn't still look like you could eat dirt, but you do. What's the matter?" Bridget asked.

"I've got a decision to make and it's not going to be easy and . . ."

"Does it have anything to do with Quincy or Baxter?" Alice asked.

Catherine plopped down in a rocker and set it in fast motion. "Yes, it does."

She told them about the ride home and Quincy's offer, ending with, "I can't go off on a lark like that and leave you to take care of this place, just the two of you."

"Don't you be making us feel all guilty," Bridget said. "Business has been steadily slowing down and we can take care of it if you want to go. It's your call and you aren't going to make us feel bad if you stay home. And if you don't go, you're not pouting around for two weeks, either. Go or put a smile on your face."

Alice picked up her brush and began to paint. "I'll tell everyone in town that you've gone to see Elizabeth in her new home. They'll believe it."

"It's a lie."

"Yep, and we really don't know where Ralph is, do we? That's the truth?" Alice said.

Catherine planted her feet on the floor and stopped the chair. "Are you blackmailing me?"

"No, I'm trying to get you not to worry

213

about people or their ideas. I don't. Folks think I'm light in the brain but I really don't give a damn. Sometimes I act that way just because I think it's funny," Alice said.

"Well, good grief," Bridget said.

"I'll think on it. What do we need to do to get ready for supper? Oh, I found the cutest little sugar shakers. You're going to love them. No more broken sugar bowl lids. I ordered one for every table in the dining room plus a few extra in case of breakage. The lid is metal but the container itself is glass. The fancy hotel where I stayed had them on the breakfast table this morning in their restaurant. And look what I brought you," Catherine talked to avoid facing the issue of Quincy as she opened her suitcase.

"How cute," Bridget squealed. "I'll make her a little pink checked dress to go with it. Just four more months and she'll be here. I can hardly wait."

"That's going to look funny on a boy," Alice said.

"It's a girl," Catherine and Bridget said at the same time.

"I brought you an Old Maid card deck." Catherine handed them over to Alice.

"Well, thank you. Now I can beat the socks off both of you. But not until after supper. Oh look at the picture of Golfer Mc-

Caddie. He looks a little like Ira, don't you think?"

"Whatever made you think of him?" Bridget asked.

"Why, this picture. It does look like him, all gangly with arms that are too long."

"Ira did kind of look like that," Catherine said. Her heart didn't skip a beat; her hands didn't go clammy; her tongue didn't stick to the roof of her mouth. They'd been engaged and yet thinking of him brought forth no emotions except a faint hint of sadness that an old friend was dead.

After unpacking her suitcase she went to the kitchen to make sure everything was ready for whatever supper rush they might have. Two sides battled as she thought about the decision to go or not. She'd never seen the ocean. Part of her wanted to lie on the sand and watch the water but that was the stuff fairy tales were made of. The practical side that said young women, even those at nearly twenty two years, did not go running off with a man just because he asked her.

She was still undecided when she went to sleep but dawn found her packing two suitcases. At nine thirty Alice drove her to the station and told her to have a good time. It was strange the way her sisters had accepted such a socially unaccepted thing as her going to the coast with Quincy. The whole morning had been surreal and she still had doubts that she'd have the nerve to board the train. She sat down on a bench and stared at it. Thousands and thousands of pounds of steel on wheels waiting to carry her off to a castle in the air but with all the subterfuge could she trust Quincy?

Mabel sat down right beside her. "Well, Catherine, where are you off to this morning?"

"Just a few days away. What are you doing down here?" Catherine asked and had to consciously not roll her eyes. This must be her punishment for being catty to Pastor Dan. The Lord did indeed work in strange ways.

"I just put my niece on the train. She was up in Little Rock visiting her mother who is my sister and stopped by here last night. Today she'll be getting on home to Shreveport. I could take you in and introduce you so you'd have someone to ride with," Mabel offered.

"Thank you but I need to purchase my ticket and that will take a few minutes," she said.

Mabel followed her to the ticket counter. "I'll keep you company while you do. I know how it is sitting in a station. It's quite boring."

"Avalon Beach, Florida. Round trip, open end," Catherine said.

"Now who do you know in Florida? That's a long way for a young woman to be traveling alone. Mercy me, but you O'Shea girls are a nervy bunch. First Bridget and her problems and now you running off to Florida all alone. Are you sure this is the right thing for you to do? I heard Pastor Dan came to see you last night and left in a huff. Was he asking you something important?"

"No he was telling me not to play cards with my sisters," Catherine said.

"You shouldn't be playing cards. They will be the ruination of the country. You mark my words. People playing such silly games when they should be doing something profitable."

Like spreading gossip, Catherine thought but held her tongue.

Mabel narrowed her eyes. "You didn't answer me. Who are you going to see in Avalon Beach?"

"Elizabeth. She and her husband have invited me for a few days," Catherine answered. "Now if you will excuse me, I have to get on the train. Elizabeth would be very disappointed if I missed it."

Mabel crossed her arms over her chest and narrowed her eyes. Those O'Shea girls were the epitome of the evils of the country. Everything was going to the devil in a hand basket. Women running around in skirt tails up above their ankles. And overalls. They were britches no matter what they called them. And the good book said women were not to be wearing men's clothing or they'd be an abomination unto the lord.

She turned quickly and headed over to Annabel's house to tell her about Catherine riding a train all the way to Florida by herself. Of course Annabel would remind her that her niece did the same thing, but Phoebe was married and had six kids. She wasn't a single, unmarried woman.

Quincy avoided Mabel even though he saw her walking away from the station. He sat down on the bench and waited until the very last call. His heart was heavy as he boarded the train. He'd hoped against all reasonable hope that she'd be there. He needed a few days with her in a setting with no outside influence. In two weeks he would have either gotten her out of his mind and heart for good or else put her there permanently. Now he'd never know.

The porter had already taken his luggage to the private car he'd booked but he didn't want to go there; not now. Later, he'd curl up on the fancy bed and reclaim some of the sleep he'd lost the night before, but right then he'd just find a seat and watch Huttig disappear through the window.

He slid into a seat and sighed. Then he realized who was sitting directly across from him.

"What took you so long?" Catherine asked.

Chapter Thirteen

Quincy swept back the window curtains so they could watch the scenery. He'd booked similar rooms before and this one wasn't better or worse. A bit smaller but he'd only asked for half a car instead of a whole one. Had they been traveling farther he'd have requested larger accommodations but they'd be at the beach by daylight.

Catherine tried to take in everything with one glance. A full sized bed with a dark green velvet spread edged with gold ball trim took most of the space on one wall. The same dark green in the form of watered silk covered the walls and lamp shades. Two overstuffed mint green chairs with matching ottomans were arranged in the middle of the room in front of a sofa on the opposite wall. A small dining table with two chairs was positioned right below the windows. It was fancier than anything she'd ever seen and it intimidated her.

That made her angry. Nothing or no one intimidated Catherine.

"What do you think? A little more comfortable than wooden seats?" He asked.

"Is this the honeymoon suite or what?" She asked right back, sharpness in her tone.

"Not hardly. That would be a full car with champagne in a glass bucket and chocolates on the table."

She sank down into one of the chairs. "And how do you know so much about it?"

"Ask me no questions, I'll tell you no lies," he grinned.

"But I thought that's what this trip was all about, other than rest and relaxation. To get to know each other. So how do I know you without asking questions?"

He got comfortable in the other chair. "Are you sure you're not a witch?"

"An Irish one. My ancestors had tall black hats and brewed potions made of eagle claws and frog legs in cauldrons," she said.

"Ahhh, that explains what I mistook for clairvoyance," he said.

"So what now?" She asked. She'd like to answer her own question. Temptation in a form much more deadly than a package of Old Maid cards sat not two feet from her. She'd like 'what now' to be a quick trip across the bridge between them, curl up in his lap and see if his kisses still sent her swirling into a puddle of desire or if it had been the affects of the storm that night.

"Get to know each other, huh? Then we shall do just that. We'll each get ten questions between now and the time we get to the end of the trip. Choose them wisely. You can have ten and I get ten but we have to agree to answer them truthfully," he said.

"What happens if we don't want to answer because it's embarrassing?"

"Then you forfeit one of your questions."

"Fair enough. I'll go first. What is the real truth about your past life?"

"Let's see, I gave you the Tonkawa story, didn't I? And the spy in the service story? So the truth? I was born and raised in Little Rock. My parents are Albert and Martha Massey. I'm an only child. My father founded a detective agency. It's very elite and very, very good. He and my mother both worked in it for many years as the only detectives. Then after I was born they hired a few men to help and expanded so that now it covers several states and employees many men and women. I went into the work when I finished college. When we entered the war I tried to enlist but the government had a different job for me. I worked as a spy. I spent two years over seas and when I came home the incident with your brother-in-law — see I didn't say his name so I haven't broken my word — was my first case back in the country. You know the rest."

"Will it be using one of my questions if I ask about your parents?" She asked.

"I'll give you that one. Bet you're wondering about my mother being a detective aren't you?"

She nodded.

"She's good at her job but after I was born she went into the bookkeeping end of the business. Now she has four employees who work for her alone. She and my father would love to retire. I've been groomed to take over the business in a year or two. I learned the whole thing from the ground floor up so I would know every aspect."

"Your mother has always worked then?"

"All my life. Consider her the first lady of women's lib. Remember she didn't just work in the office for my father, she was a real detective. The reason we have a house in Avalon Beach is because they were there doing some work concerning a smuggling business almost thirty years ago. To be exact, it was twenty nine years ago last month. I was born in the house and they closed a very high paying, very secretive case right there. So they used part of the money and bought the house. It's been one of our vacation homes ever since."

Nine questions left. She'd have to think on them a while so she wouldn't waste one.

"My turn," he said. "As you know I'm already acquainted with your past from the reports I've read. That's why I've allowed you to ask a few extras concerning my parents."

"Hey, I'm not in debt to you for that," she bristled.

"Don't be getting your hackles up," he said.

"Don't tell me what or what not to do."

"Bit of a spit fire aren't you?" He snapped right back at her.

"I live up to my red hair," she answered with a smile.

That threw him off balance. He expected her to come back with another acidic remark, not flash him a lovely smile. The next two weeks should be very interesting. One thing for sure, she'd keep him on his toes. It wouldn't be boring.

"Okay, then, question one. Have you ever been in love?"

Whew! That one took her by complete surprise. Something that serious should have been question ninety nine or five hundred, not the very first one. "Can I think about that one for a while?" She asked.

"Is that your second question?"

"You aren't playing fair."

"Then phrase your answer in something other than a question, and no, I want the first thing off the top of your head, not a well thought out evasive answer. So the question stands, have you ever been in love?"

She licked her lips and frowned. "I've been engaged and he died. You already know that."

"That's not what I asked."

"No, I have not been in love. I admired Ira. He was a hard working man, respectable, kind, gentle. He would have made a fine husband and father, but I did not love him." She answered honestly without looking at him. But by golly, she knew now that she could ask personal questions and he'd best get ready for some of those 'off the top of his head' answers, also.

"Why?" He asked.

"Is that question two?"

"No, I withdraw it."

Before either one could ask another question someone rapped on the door. Quincy arose and slung the door wide open to allow the porter to roll in their lunch. He'd ordered both meals for the day and an evening snack to be brought to the car before they went to sleep that night. He tipped the man and brought the cart into the room, parking it between them.

"Hope you are hungry. I didn't eat much breakfast." He didn't tell her that he was too nervous to eat but that his appetite had returned with vengeance.

"What is . . . I mean . . . that is not a question. I'll open the lids myself and find out what is under there," she said.

"Now you are learning." He picked up the dome shaped covers and revealed chicken breasts on rice with fresh asparagus on the side. A white linen napkin covered a basket of hot rolls. A bowl of fresh fruit topped with whipped cream and crushed pecans was under a crystal lid. A platter of cookies had been set off to one side; gingersnaps, sugar with icing and lemon thins. A tall crystal pitcher of lemonade and a carafe of coffee waited to be poured.

"It looks scrumptious," she said.

"Shall we . . . I mean we will eat at the table. I'll transfer it from the cart and we can watch the scenery as we dine," he said.

"Now you are learning." She shot his own line right back at him.

She was amazed at the quality of the food. When she'd ridden the train to El Dorado and eaten in the dining room car, the food had been passable but nothing extraordinary. Evidently if a person had connections and money, they could purchase most anything.

"So my turn. Number two. Right back at you. Have you ever been in love?" She asked as she buttered a roll. "And if I can't think about it, neither can you. Honesty, remember."

"I've pretended to be in love many times for the job's sake. I thought I was in love with Laura White and mooned over her for three months. But then she moved away and I found another girlfriend who was in my fourth grade class. Laura was one of those older women. She was probably fifteen and I was nine. Then there was Lucinda when I was a teenager but that could be classified infatuation instead of love. And when I was twenty there was Millie. I was going through my knight-in-shining armor days. Her boyfriend had eloped with her best friend and she was in deep distress. I jumped on my white horse and rode off to rescue her. I courted her for about a month and I was ready to ask her to marry me but my mother finally put me on a kitchen chair and had a long talk with me. She asked me the same question in different words that you just did. 'Are you in love with Millie or do you feel sorry for her because she's been wronged?' I had to be honest then, too. So I guess my answer is no, I have not truly been in love."

"That was a heck of a long explanation when a simple no would have done the trick," she said.

"I was talking out loud and examining all my past women," he said.

"All?"

"Is that a question?"

"I withdraw," she said. He'd mentioned three women. She doubted if that was all he'd known in twenty–nine years. He knew his way around the kissing game so well it proved without wasting a question that he'd been with far more than a measly three.

"This is excellent food. I wonder . . . no, I'll rephrase . . . I'd like to know what they marinated the chicken in. We could serve it at the Black Swan."

"I don't think so. Your clientele depend on the same things on the same days. Major told me that's what made the Swan so special. You always knew what you were getting and it was always good."

"Boring, more like it. Papa was of the same mind as Major. Give them good food in a pleasant setting and they'd come back for more. It worked but Momma would have liked to show off her skills. She was a wonderful cook. Sometimes she made special meals just for the family and we'd eat after clean up in the evenings."

"Aha, I got a bit of information without asking," he said.

"Think you're sneaky, don't you." She chewed slowly trying to determine what was in the sauce but didn't have a bit of luck.

"My next question and rules of the game say that after today we only get five each day that we are on the shore," he said.

"Who made the rules . . . oops, retraction." She rephrased it several times but couldn't figure out a way to ask without a question.

"I don't think I'm sneaky. I know it. That's what makes a good detective, my lady. My question is — did you ever resent being so tied down to one place?"

"No, I did not. If you never have chocolate bars you don't miss them. I was only five when we moved to Huttig. I don't remember much about the place we left except that it had open fields and lots of room for Momma's garden and for me to run and play. But Momma made a lovely home for us in Huttig. We knew everyone and we never thought about anyplace else."

"I'll give you a bit without a question. I've traveled everywhere. First with my parents when they were on a job. They could pose as a family and no one suspects a married couple with a child to be doing undercover work. Then by myself when I got older. Sometimes with Elizabeth if I needed a lady in my life. She's a good detective. She and her new husband will most likely follow in my parent's footsteps for a few years before the children arrive."

"Did she . . . wow, this is hard . . . Elizabeth wrote us a letter explaining the situation and gave us permission to tell Mabel," Catherine said.

"I know. I read it. It was a real hoot, wasn't it? That girl should be a writer. Knowing Mabel's love for gossip I bet it worked like a charm."

"You are right. It did work. I told Mabel all of it, plus the fact Bridget was divorced and expecting a baby all the same afternoon. Almost gave her gossip indigestion," Catherine laughed.

It was music to his ears. It wasn't a school girl giggle or a chuckle but a full fledged laugh from the pit of her soul. And it was infectious.

He laughed with her.

She dried her eyes on the linen napkin

and laid it aside. "It was so funny. I thought she'd blow a gasket for sure before she got out of the house and back to her bridge club. She might be queen of the gossip vine club for a whole year with all that. I don't know of a single lady who could top it for quantity. Now, quality is a different matter since one third of it was pure bull crap."

She helped herself to a sugar cookie and a bowl of fruit. "So five questions a day will be the limit. I'll have to write them down and make sure I don't waste any."

He bypassed the fruit and picked up a cookie of each variety. "I'll do the same. How about . . . you're right . . . this isn't easy. I'd never noticed how much we depend on questions in every day conversation."

"I'm not at all sleepy. I might read a book I brought along. You go ahead and take a nap. By the way, how are we . . ."

"I know what you are about to ask. I shall take the sofa tonight and you are having the bed. I said I would be a gentleman. But since you aren't sleepy at this time, I'll nap on the bed and you can read on the sofa."

"Thank you," she mumbled.

He loaded the dishes back onto the cart, leaving the cookies and coffee in the middle of the table. "I'll push this out and lock the door. Wake me if you think of an important question."

He removed his suit jacket and vest, slipped off his tie, kicked off his shoes and stretched out on top of the bedspread. In moments he'd turned on his right side, pulled the other pillow from under the spread and hugged it. He was sound asleep within five minutes.

Catherine drank in the sight of him without having to look away. His black hair was thick, combed back, a little longer than most men wore theirs. Dark eyelashes rested on high cheek bones and a strong chin was tucked into the pillow. His shirt sleeves were filled with muscular arms extending down to thick fingers that looked more like a mill workers hands instead of a desk worker.

The sight of him caused her to breathe a little faster so she shut her eyes and turned away from him. She took a book from her suitcase and stretched out on the extra long sofa. Before she finished page one her chin had dropped to her chest. Quincy snored and startled her awake. She already had her legs propped up and her shoes off so she removed the pins from her hair, shook out a mane of burgundy that reached past her waist and laid her head back on the overstuffed sofa arm. The last thing she remembered as she shut her eyes was thinking that she'd only rest for a moment. Quincy must not awake and find her with her hair down.

He did. He stretched all six feet plus of his height getting the kinks out and then looked around the room for Catherine. She was asleep with a book on the floor beside her. He eased out of bed and pulled one of the chairs a little closer so he could sit and stare as long as he wanted. His hands itched to touch that mass of red hair. His lips twitched wanting to kiss her awake. The temptation to simply run his fingertips down her finely boned jaw was almost more than he could bear.

She opened her eyes to find him only inches from her, his brown eyes dreamy. She would have liked to reach up and drag his lips to hers. He had promised to be a gentleman but she hadn't made any such vow about staying a respectable lady. She hesitated and the moment passed.

"Wake up Sleeping Beauty," he said.

She remembered her hair. Momma was adamant about keeping their hair up once they put on long skirts. Although she was a forerunner for women's rights on some issues, she maintained until her dying day that a woman should keep her hair up like a lady. Only questionable women ran around with their hair flying in their faces.

"Oh, no!" Catherine grabbed her pins and hastily twisted it up into a bun near the top of her head.

"I liked it down," Quincy said.

"According to the fairy tale, the handsome prince kissed Sleeping Beauty to wake her. You just stared me awake," she ignored his remark about her hair.

"Disappointed?" He asked.

"Question?"

"Retracted. I'll waste one, though. What would you have done if I had kissed you awake?"

"Kissed you back, but the moment has passed and I am fully awake. That's three for you, Quincy."

"I shall let my mind rule next time rather than my heart," he declared.

Chapter Fourteen

Catherine could smell the difference in the air when they stepped off the train. Palm trees, some as tall as the pine trees in Arkansas, waved slightly to the north. The south wind brought the salty aroma of the ocean and lured her to come and see. She and Quincy were the only ones who left the train; none got on.

"Ivan!" Quincy yelled at a man getting out of a pickup truck not far from where they stood beside their luggage.

He crossed the space and shook hands with Quincy. "Hello."

"This is Catherine O'Shea. And this is Ivan. He takes care of the house on the beach for us and is kind enough to get up early to come get us." He made introductions and explained.

"I'm pleased to meet you," Catherine said.

" 'Tis my pleasure, my lady," Ivan's bright blue eyes sparkled. His red hair was the color of Alice's and matched his beard. His face was square and his nose bulbous. His shoulders wide and his arms big enough to carry a fifty foot pine tree across town.

He picked up four suitcases as if they held nothing but chicken feathers. "Well, let's get all this in the back of the truck and get you settled. Birdy went in yesterday and got the place ready. I made sure the bicycles had air in the tires. There's food in the house so you should be all right for today."

Quincy gathered up the rest of the luggage and followed him. "So how's the fishin' been?"

"We've had a good year. I'm runnin' three shrimp boats now. Birdy is wantin' me to cut back on the hours but I'm a workin' man. I'll drop in my tracks the day after I bring in a record amount and die a happy man. If I was sittin' home all day with nothing to do, I'd be dead in a week. Now, you crawl right in here between me and Quincy, Miss Catherine. It's not too far to the house. Did Quincy tell you about it?"

She was wedged between two men in a rattling truck with rusted fenders and no glass in the front window and barely had time to shake her head in answer.

"Well, it's rough compared to city living. We ain't got electricity in these parts yet,

236

nor any of that indoor plumbing either. Never did see what Quincy loved about it so much. Lives like a king up there in Arkansas and comes down here when he has time off. If I had two weeks I wouldn't be coming to this place, that's for sure," Ivan talked as he drove.

Catherine had trouble keeping her nostrils from flaring at the thought of such an ordeal. *Great God, what have I gotten myself into? No electricity. No bathroom. I thought I was going on a vacation. Looks like I was wrong.*

Five minutes later he pulled up to a small white house, no bigger than the saw mill houses in Huttig.

"Here we are. I'll help you get these bags on the screened porch and then I'm going to work. Birdy said to tell you hello. Come around if you get lonely in this forsaken place."

There was no wooden door into the screened porch, just one made of the same fine screen as they'd used to enclose the porch to keep the mosquitoes at bay. Quincy helped Ivan unload the baggage. Then Ivan left and they were alone.

The porch had two rockers that had many coats of white paint on them. They had wide arms and an oil lamp on a table between them. A soft, gentle breeze flowed unhindered through the screen. Catherine entertained notions of sitting out there in the evening reading a book by the light of the lamp. Quincy opened the back door with a key he fished from his pocket and motioned her inside.

"You are in the kitchen, as you can see. The stove works and there's an ice box, no fancy refrigerator. The ice man will bring us a chunk every morning. Ivan will have taken care of that for today already." He opened the oak ice box to show her a huge square of ice already melting into the pan under it.

He opened the metal cabinets to reveal dishes, pots and pans and food. "Not much matches anymore but it's usable," he said.

Wallpaper covered with yellow daisies and bright white cabinets brought warmth into the kitchen. On the other end of the elongated room, a small table and four chairs were placed under a window that looked out over the beach. She couldn't take her eyes from the white sand or the water. If the house had no other room in it, she wouldn't care. She looked forward to breakfast in the early morning when dawn chased away the darkness of night.

"There's more," Quincy took her arm.

She wasn't ready for the effect of his bare

hand on her skin. Sparks rippled up and down her body, starting at her forearm and ending at her toes.

He led her through a doorway into the living area. All the walls were painted white and the front door opened out onto a porch with steps straight to the sand. Forget the window. She'd have breakfast out there on the porch and start every morning with the smell of salt in her nose. An overstuffed parlor suit upholstered in faded blue tapestry filled the room. There was a large sofa on one wall, a table and hurricane lamp separating it from a large arm chair on one side and a matching table, lamp arrangement on the other with a parlor chair on the other side of that. Two more parlor chairs were place in front of the window with a third table and lamp between them. A small hallway at the north end of the living room led to two bedrooms.

"You can have first choice. This one is only a bit smaller," he said.

"I want the one that has a window facing the water," she said quickly.

"They both do. You can have the larger one. It has two sides with windows so you can have a view straight ahead and one with the sun coming up in the other one," he said.

She loved the room. She didn't care if there was no indoor plumbing or electricity. Bright rays of sun filtered through sheer lacy curtains covering enormous windows on the east. There was an oak bed, fairly plain with only a bit of ornate work on the six foot headboard. The square dresser had a mirror on one side and a towel bar on the other. A washbowl and pitcher with a blue floral design waited for use. The south wall had a window and a door opening out onto the porch. She slung it open and inhaled deeply.

"I may run away from home and live here forever," she said.

Quincy had been afraid she'd turn tail and catch the first train back north when she saw the place. He'd always loved it on the shore, found the simplicity refreshing and relaxing, but he'd had second thoughts about bringing Catherine to such a remote area after he'd asked her.

"Five questions a day. I was about to ask you what you'd like for breakfast. Maybe we'd better see what's in the ice box," he said.

"Can we . . . no, let's eat out on the porch and then can we . . . no, we will go wading in the water," she said.

"Sounds good to me. Let's make scrambled egg sandwiches. We'll keep it pretty simple since it's your vacation, too. I don't expect you to cook all that much and I'm not much of a cook," he said.

They sliced into one of two large loaves of fresh bread and cracked half a dozen eggs into a bowl. Ivan had started a fire in the stove earlier that morning so it was already hot and the eggs cooked quickly. They carried plates and mugs filled with hot coffee to the porch where two oak rockers waited. Both chairs had worn arms, testimony to the many times they'd been used in almost thirty years.

Catherine balanced her plate on her knees and sipped coffee while she waited on the eggs to cool.

"You'll want to change into your overall things," he said.

She nodded, afraid that words would take away the serenity.

"We'll take a long walk down the shoreline. You can collect sea shells if you like," he said.

She nodded again.

"Mercy, I didn't know the sight would render you speechless," he teased.

"Hush. I don't want to miss a single sound of the water or the birds or the wind," she said.

After they finished eating, she unpacked

and changed from her traveling dress into a pair of chambray overalls. Stockings in hand, she glanced out at the sand. How did she phrase a question without actually making it one?

He called through the hallway. "I'm going barefoot. Sand just gets in your socks and shoes and it's easier to go without either."

She tossed the stockings on the bed. She opened the door from her bedroom out onto the porch and stepped out. She wore plain blue overalls, a white cotton blouse with three-quarter sleeves and had braided her hair into two long ropes she'd wrapped around her head like a crown.

He joined her, wearing khaki trousers and a white shirt with the sleeves rolled up to his elbows. His feet were long, narrow and very pale.

"Let's go get some sand between our toes," he said.

"I'm more than ready. Would it be . . . no, I'm not wasting a question on that . . . I'm going to roll the legs of my overalls up and wade in that water. If it's going to create a problem or if it's a sin in these parts then you better get ready to shut your eyes or else pray for my soul."

"Amazing how hard conversations are when you have to watch how many questions you ask." He led the way down the stairs and out onto sand so white and fine it resembled sugar.

Sea oats grew in clumps behind drift wood or out in the open. Pelicans and sand pipers flew in and out, gathering food for the day. The sky was brilliant blue without a cloud in sight. The ocean rushed forward bringing all kinds of shells, then back again to scoop up more. Catherine could imagine Alice with her sketch pad. With all that wide open space, she could set her easel up on the porch or right out in the sand and paint without sketches.

"Hey, we forgot the bag," he said before they reached the bottom step. He ran back inside the house, returning with a bag made of crocheted webbing. "For the shells," he explained.

Her face and eyes were a question.

"It's made from an old fish net Ivan had. We've got several of them. They're great for collecting clams or shells. We'll wait until evening and dig for clams. Ivan has put milk in the ice box so we can have chowder."

"He mentioned bicycles," she said about the same time her feet hit the sand. To her surprise it was soft. She wiggled her toes in the warmth and gasped at the sensation.

"I've been coming here forever. I can't

imagine as an adult not having ever put my feet in warm sand. It must be a wonderful thing," he said.

"You did it without asking me how much I like it. I'll tell you since you are so good at this game. It's absolutely delightful. There are no words to describe it. I may bring my pillow out here and sleep in the sand."

"You'll have a time washing it from your hair. Look. There's a perfect conch shell."

Their fingers grabbed at the same time. She jumped as if she'd been burned; he kept his hand clasped around hers another few seconds, enjoying not only the sparks but also the way she'd reacted. For the first time he realized that the kisses they'd shared had affected her the same way they did him.

He pulled his hand away and let her pick it up. "Put it to your ear. You can hear the ocean in it."

She did. "How does it do that?"

"You're the Irish witch. You tell me."

"It's a gift. The goddess of the ocean knows we mere mortals can't live forever on the beach so she lets this be washed up on the shore for us to carry home. Then when we are sad and lonely we can put it to our ear and have the memory of our first day to walk on the sand."

"I don't know about an Irish witch, but I

believe you kissed the blarney stone right on the lips," he said.

She swatted at the air close to his arm, careful not to touch his skin again. "I'll carry it. It might get broken in that bag."

He remembered something she'd said earlier. "You said something about Ivan telling me the bicycles were ready. They are our means of transportation. We don't have a car. Town is a mile away. There's a small store and post office combination. It's a bakery, butcher, general merchandise place. So starting tomorrow, we'll ride into town each morning and pick up the day's supplies. They also have post cards there if you want to send one to your sisters."

"But not today. This day let's just be hermits."

"Question one for the day. You've lived with people all around you your whole life. Why does this appeal to you?" He asked.

Because you are here with me. Because I really like you, Quincy, even though these two weeks will most likely be all we ever have. Because if we got really serious about each other and you proposed to me, I'd have to tell you about Ralph because married people don't have secrets. Or do they? Did Momma have a few secrets from Daddy? I'll have to think about that.

"Maybe because it is so very different. I never knew any other kind of life. Even when Momma died and we had to shut the hotel for three weeks, the knowledge that it would open again was still there. Here, it's like heaven. No responsibilities. Just peace and quiet the way God intended it. I had never given the idea of going to see the ocean a thought but now I'll miss it when I go home. There may be nights when I sleep with this shell on my pillow. Maybe because it's the Irish in me and my ancestors were fishermen and it's in my blood to love the water. Whatever makes this appeal to me has a strong hold on me."

"Someday you will have to travel to Ireland. It's a place of green beauty," he said.

"Nothing could ever be this lovely. Not even my father's mother country."

She meandered closer to the water's edge, letting it slosh up on her bare feet.

"I'm going swimming later. You might like to try it." He chose his words carefully.

"I can swim like an otter in a creek. I can not imagine swimming in this." The water swirled around her ankles wetting the cuffs of her overalls.

"You can join me," he said.

"I did not bring a swimming suit. Don't own one. Momma only let us girls swim with each other and then it was in our oldest, most rattiest, chemise and bloomer combination. She'd turn over in her grave if she heard me discussing such a thing with a man," Catherine smiled.

"I won't tell. No swimming suit. Hmmm. We shall have to remedy that," he said.

She glanced up to see an evil glint in his eye and immediately read his thoughts. "Oh, no, you will not . . ." She began to walk backward and then turned on a dime and ran as hard as she could.

The sand and the fear of dropping her prize shell slowed her down. Her legs were long and her strides even longer but he caught up with her in less than a hundred feet. He scooped her up into his arms like a bride and waded out into the water.

"Put me down. You're going to break my shell," she screamed.

He carefully took it from her hands, carried her back to the shore where he'd dropped the bag and laid the shell on top of it, all without letting go of Catherine. Then it was back out into the ocean until he was waist deep, at which time he dropped her — bottom first into the waves.

She squealed and came up coughing and giggling at the same time. "I love it. It's so warm. Let's swim all the way out to where we can't touch bottom."

"You are a good sport," he said.

"I can't be mad at you for giving me exactly what I wanted but was afraid I'd never get." She kicked off toward deeper water.

Half an hour later they were stretched out on the sand, starving but too tired to walk back to the house and fix lunch. He lay on his back, eyes shut, wet shirt sticking to every muscle. She propped up on a hip and an elbow and admired his body. At first glance she'd thought he was tall and gangly like Ira, but now she realized his arms were muscular, his stomach hard and flat. And from what she could see through the soaking shirt there was a bed of fine furry hair on his chest.

"Liking what you see?" He asked.

"You are supposed to be asleep. Is that question number two for the day?"

He opened his eyes. "I'm not and it is so answer it."

"Are you demanding?"

"Is that a question?"

"Retracted. Okay, yes, I do like what I was seeing. You are a very handsome man."

"I'm far too serious and my chin is too strong," he said.

"That's your opinion. Mine differs. I'm

starving. Let's go make lunch and get out of these wet clothes. I suppose I'll have to wash my hair to get the ocean water out of it," she said.

"It's really not the ocean. It's the Gulf of Mexico," he said.

"It's salty so it's the ocean. Argument closed. I shall always remember it as the ocean. If you look out there there's nothing but water and sky. That's the ocean to me. Now, let's go find something to eat before I wilt away to nothing." She retrieved her shell and headed back.

"I like what I see, too. Nice . . . ahem . . . outfit," he raised his eyebrows rakishly.

"You are a rogue. You promised to be a gentleman."

"I will. Not once will you wake up and find me next to you. But I'm not blind," he teased.

"I'm too tall and have red hair and my eyes are a nondescript green. There's nothing nice about me," she said.

"That's your opinion. Mine differs," he said.

Lunch was two thick slabs of bread slathered with fresh churned butter, half inch slices of sugar cured ham, lettuce and tomatoes and boiled eggs. They had lemonade with their sandwiches and nothing had ever tasted so good to Catherine.

He was flirting with me, she thought. *Men folks don't talk to ladies like that, but then real ladies don't go off on a lark with a man on a moment's notice. I guess Mabel was right. The O'Shea girls are a wild bunch of women.*

"I would love to know what you are thinking," he said.

"I was wondering how to wash my hair," she lied.

"We've got a pump in the kitchen. We'll heat some water and fill a basin. You can lean over it and I'll do the soaping and rinsing."

"I suppose if I'm going to swim, it'll have to be done every day," she mused.

"That's right. Mother said it was the payment for a good time but Father always helped her. I watched so I know how to do it."

The O'Shea sisters already had the wild name so she might as well act that way. It sounded absolutely delicious to have Quincy wash her hair. No one had done that since she had been six years old back when her mother did it for her.

She finished her lunch and began removing pins from two long wet braids hanging on either side of her bosom all the way past her waist. "Then let's get at it. Afterward,

I'll clean up and wash the salt out of my clothing. I'm glad I brought two pair of overalls. What time do we go clam digging?"

"Is that a question?" He grinned.

"Number one of the day and important enough to ask. I can't wait to see how it's done and to eat chowder made from fresh clams."

"We'll go at dusk," he said, amazed that his voice was even close to normal. His mouth was as dry as if he'd walked across the Sahara without a drop of water at the sight of her taking those long ropey braids apart.

Chapter Fifteen

The wind blew across Catherine's face, keeping errant strands of hair that insisted on coming loose from the bun at the nape of her neck blown back, away from her eyes and mouth. It had been years since she'd ridden a bicycle. Alice had kept up the maintenance on their old childhood cycle and kept it in pristine condition in the tool shed. Bridget tried riding once and fell off. It was her last attempt because she skinned her elbow. She called the contraption a demon and never touched it again.

Catherine enjoyed riding along beside Quincy. She used his mother's bicycle a black Uno, the same make and model as the one they had in Huttig. Quincy rode the gent's Uno, the only difference being the bar from the handle bars to the seat and it was dark green. His folks had affixed straw baskets on the front handlebars to tote things back and forth from the market. Both were well filled that morning with long loaves of fresh baked bread, milk, shrimp so fresh that it had been wiggling a few minutes ago, two pounds of cheese and a half pound of tea.

Catherine could hardly wait to get back to the house and kick off her shoes. She planned to take a book to the beach and do nothing but enjoy the afternoon.

They leaned the bicycles next to the screened porch and she helped carry in the day's supply of groceries.

"Work is over. Play begins," he said. "We'll have sandwiches for lunch and I'll make boiled shrimp and red sauce for supper. It's either that or scampi or both if we're hungry. Add a pot of rice and we'll dine in fine style. I'm thinking of a long, lazy afternoon on the beach."

"You're getting really good at talking without questions," she said. "I'm going to grab my book and head for the sand."

"I'll bring a quilt and umbrella," he said.

She cocked her head to one side and her eyebrows drew just slightly downward.

He chuckled.

"That's no fair. Asking a question without a word but I'll answer it. The quilt is so we don't have sand all over us. The umbrella is to keep the afternoon sun off your face so you won't freckle."

"Question one for this day," she said. "Do you think freckles are abominable?"

"No, I think they're endearing but most women with a complexion like yours would die before they'd entice the sun to make freckles, and besides, the umbrella will provide a little shade. It can get warm out there in the afternoon," he said.

"Then I'll go swimming and cool off, but bring the umbrella because I don't want wrinkles around my eyes from squinting in the hot sun to see the print in my book," she said.

She kept her feet off the end of the quilt and in the warm sand, sitting with her knees drawn up and book open on them as she read. Or at least pretended to read. The steady ocean breeze kept wafting the aroma of his shaving lotion from the other side of the quilt where he lay on his stomach, book open before him, turning pages periodically.

She looked at his book and was amazed. "You are reading *Tom Sawyer.*"

"Is that a question? No of course it isn't. Yes, I'm reading *Tom Sawyer.* I know it's supposed to be for kids but I read it for the first time when I was here as a little boy and it's tradition. I read it every time I get back down here and every time I discover something new."

"I love that book," she said.

"Then you can read it when I finish. I'll read yours," he said.

She laughed.

"Then I won't read yours."

She nodded.

"Never did get into love stories. Give me a good war time or humorous book," he said.

She stretched out on her back, lacing her fingers behind her head and staring ahead. "Tell me about Florida. I'm thinking about selling the hotel and moving here."

"Then you'll probably want to move over on the east coast. There's lots of development going on over there these days. A real boom in land. This side will catch up. In fifty years it will be nothing but hotels and places to accommodate tourists coming down here for the mild weather and beaches. My father has bought quite a lot of beach front property. Says it's a wise investment. He doesn't plan to do one thing with it but wait until the big tourist thing creates a bigger boom. The temperature is mild here all the time. Gets a little nippy in the winter, but further on south down at the tip of the state and in the Keys, it's balmy most of the time. They've just recently created a citrus growers organization. Oranges, grapefruit, limes and lemons are sent out of the state by the train load. Those trains that brought soldiers down here for training in the Navy were originally put there to take fruit and fish out of the state to other places. That's why one comes so close to Avalon Beach. It's a shrimping area. Ivan makes a good living at shrimping."

"Interesting. Then would your father sell me this place right here to put a hotel?"

"Number two of the day?"

"That's it and I'm serious," she said.

"Your sisters would never leave Huttig. Alice is comfortable there. Bridget is having a baby."

"I know, but today I'm dreaming." She yawned, shut her eyes and fell asleep.

He propped himself up on one elbow and stared. He was in love with the woman and keeping his hands to himself wasn't easy, but he'd given his word and he'd abide by it.

"In love," he whispered almost inaudibly.

I can't be in love with her. I really thought I'd bring her here and get rid of any attraction I've had for her, not admit love. Good Lord, what would Mother and Daddy say? In love? Me? Who cares what they say? It's my life and my heart and why am I arguing with myself. Even if I were in love with Catherine she would never fall for me because of the thing that lies between us. Ralph Contiello. She can't tell me the whole truth and I could never live with a woman without sharing everything with her like my parents do.

She was alone on the quilt when she opened her eyes. He came toward her from the south end of the beach and the closer he got the more she could see the aggravation in his posture and face. His back was ramrod straight and sand kicked up behind his feet as he walked. His brow was knit in a solid line and the muscles of his jaws worked as he gritted his teeth.

She sat up when he got closer. "I'll waste my third one. What happened while I was asleep that put you in a mood?"

"I'd have thought an Irish witch would know," he smarted off.

So it had taken less than two days for familiarity to breed contempt.

"No hateful come backs?" He asked.

"Question?"

"I want an answer and I'm tired of this silly game," he said.

"No hateful comebacks and you are the one who started the silly game. It was fun and I'll hate to see it end but it can be over. What my intuition says is that we've been

257

together too much. It's time for you to go away. Go fishing with Ivan or we'll draw up some lines in the sand and you stay on one side and I'll stay on the other. Either that or I'll pack my suitcases and you can call Ivan to take me to the train station. I have an open end ticket. I can leave and I will. I won't stay here and be miserable. I can go home and do that," she said.

He plopped down on the quilt. "Outspoken aren't you?" The idea of her leaving left him empty. Twelve days without her would be eternity.

"I speak my mind. So do I pack or are you going fishing with Ivan tomorrow morning?"

"I'm going to go riding on my bicycle right now. Please don't pack. It's nothing you've done. It's me and I've got to work it out for myself," he said.

"Then go do it and don't come home until you've got the job done," she said.

"You'll be all right by yourself here?" He asked.

"I'm a big girl. Stay as long as you need to. If you don't get back by supper, then I'll figure you and Ivan are fishing all night. Have fun."

He stood up and walked away. In a few minutes she heard the back door slam and figured he was on his way to wherever Ivan lived. For the first time in her entire life, Catherine was totally alone and in a strange place.

Quincy changed into his fishing clothes: bibbed overalls, flannel shirt and old boots. He tossed a pair of rubber boots into the basket on his bicycle and left before he traipsed right back down to the beach and told her why he was angry. He had no right to leave her in limbo wondering if she'd done something wrong, but he couldn't tell her what the problem was before he gave it a lot more thought.

How on earth had he fallen in love with Catherine? True, he'd admit from the first there was a physical attraction. What man with good eyesight wouldn't be attracted to her? She was stunning with that burgundy hair, green eyes and skin like porcelain, not to mention those lips made for kissing, a tiny waist and full, rounded hips.

He rode on in spite of the desire to turn the bicycle around. Two miles south down a dirt road he stopped at a huge sprawling house set back a little farther from the beachfront than his place. Birdy was out in the yard hanging up clothes to dry, several small children playing chase around her.

"It's about time you come around. Where's the lady Ivan's been talking about? Says she's your cousin. I don't believe it. Tell me the truth." She clamped a pin on the last pillow case and crossed the yard in long easy strides to hug him.

"She's not my cousin," he said.

Birdy and Ivan were of an age; younger than his parents, who were forty–nine last fall; older than him by fifteen years. Their two oldest sons, Harold and Richard, were already married, hence the children playing in the yard. Their youngest two were still in high school. Ivan insisted every one of the boys have an education whether they wanted to fish or not. It took as many brains, according to his philosophy, to run a business as brawn.

Birdy was a tall woman with hair that used to be blond but was now sprinkled with gray. Her eyes were still bright blue and full of sass, her skin brown as toast from the ever blowing warm winds and her hugs still warm and friendly. She wore a calico dress that had faded blue flowers on a yellow background.

She pushed away from him. "So why are you living down there with her? You know that's a sin. Come on into the house and tell us about her. Midge and Connie are in there making pies for supper. I expect you can talk in front of them."

"I'm not living with her, Birdy. She's staying in one bedroom and me in the other. We're just getting to know each other."

Midge was Harold's wife; Connie was married to Richard. He'd known both of them as long as he'd known their husbands. They'd all five run the beaches together as small children and teenagers. He was only three years older than Harold and four years older than Richard. Midge and Connie fit in there somewhere but he wasn't exactly sure just where.

"Hey, look what I found." Birdie called out as she opened the kitchen door into a house that had started out as small as the one on the beach. But then they'd had children so they added a few rooms on the north end. Harold got married and that warranted another addition on the south end for his family. Richard followed suit and a wing off to the east was constructed.

Connie crossed the room and hugged him. "Well look what the dog has drug up."

Midge did the same. "And the cat wouldn't have."

"You look like you're ready for fishing. If you hurry you might catch them down at the dock. Harold ran up and said they had a full load and were going back for the night. They'll come in at dawn and take a rest then," Connie said.

"But first you're going to tell us about this woman," Birdy said. "I don't care if you miss the boat altogether. I'm going to have a few answers."

"She's not my cousin. She was one of the suspects in a murder case I was investigating and I've flat out fallen for her and don't know what to do," he admitted honestly.

"Who'd she kill?" Midge asked.

"If she killed anyone it was her brother-in-law for beating her sister, Bridget, who is expecting a baby," he said.

"In that case, forget the case. Sorry sucker that did that deserved to die and even God will turn a blind eye to that one," Connie said.

"Do you think she did it?" Birdy asked.

"No, I don't. But I do think she knows where the body is and the three O'Shea sisters have made a pact to never tell. I don't know if I could go into a marriage with a woman who didn't share everything with me," he said.

It started off as a snicker between Midge and Connie. It ended up as a kitchen full of laugher so loud it brought the grandchildren inside. Three women wiped at their eyes with their apron tails and tried to sip water to get rid of the hiccups.

"What is so dang funny?" Quincy asked.

"You tell Harold every thing you ever did before you married him?" Connie asked Midge.

"He married me didn't he?"

"How about you, Mother McCleary? Does Papa Ivan know every single thing you did before you vowed to be faithful the rest of your life?" Connie asked.

Birdy wiped at her eyes. "I'm still married ain't I?"

Connie shooed four children out the back door. "You kids get on back outside and play. Quincy, the the past is the past. Forget it and go on to the future. If you love this woman then don't let her get away."

"Thank you, I'm going fishing," he said abruptly and left by the same door he'd entered without understanding what was so amusing.

Catherine grew restless right after supper. She walked to the beach only to come back to the porch, sit a spell and watch the birds coming and going, then to the back screened porch to rock and wish she knew what was on Quincy's mind. She replayed the day's events. Everything had been fine when they rode into town for supplies and even when they went to the beach. Whatever happened had done so while she was sleeping. Had someone visited or brought mail. Perhaps his father was calling him home before his vacation was finished and he didn't want to tell her.

At dusk she heard an automobile coming down the road and jumped up to meet Quincy. He was about to get a piece of her mind and they'd argue for sure, he wasn't running out on her again. She was surprised when she threw open the door to find three women getting out of Ivan's old truck.

"Hi there. We've come to visit. I'm Ivan's wife, Birdy and these are my daughters-in-law, Midge, the short one and Connie the tall one. I brought cookies. You put on the coffee," she said.

Catherine was speechless for a few minutes but then found her voice. "I'm glad to meet you all."

"And surprised as the devil to see us, huh?" Connie smiled.

Even by the light from several oil lamps she could see neither of the younger women were knock-down gorgeous. Pretty with dark hair cut in one of the newer styles she'd seen in the magazines. Midge had light green eyes like Bridget's and Connie's were so deep brown they appeared to be black. Midge was rounder than Connie who was tall and lanky. It was evident that Birdy had been the pretty one when she was their age. Blue eyes flashing around the kitchen as she took plates and cups from the cabinets, making herself right at home.

Birdy pointed to the table. "Okay, come and sit while the coffee boils. We've come to see who could make Quincy act like a worm in hot ashes, so you're about to be put under the light, Catherine."

Catherine was glad for a chair. So much energy in one room was tiring. "What are you talking about?"

Connie took a cookie from the top of the stack and ate it in three easy bites. "I'll go first. God, this is nice. I'd forgotten how nice it is to have a few minutes without kids under my feet."

"Kids?" Catherine asked.

Midge grabbed a cookie. "Bit of history. I'm married to Richard, and Connie's husband is Harold. They're Ivan and Birdy's oldest set of two boys. Then there's Evan and Jessie who are about to finish their schooling and then they'll join Papa Ivan on the boats. But right now they are home taking care of our four young 'uns. I've got two boys and Connie has two girls. Basically we all live in the same house down the road a piece."

"Quincy came by today and we asked him outright if you was his cousin," Birdy said.

"I'm not," Catherine stammered.

"We know that," Birdy said.

"It's not what you think. He has a bedroom and I have one. My sisters and I run a hotel in Huttig and it's no different than having gentlemen guests . . ."

"Hey, you don't have to explain to us. But I think you're a bit touched in the head if you let rules get in the way of your heart," Connie said. "God, I would have given my right arm for a set up like this when Harold and I were courtin'."

Birdy pointed at her. "Your momma and I would have both whipped your hind ends. You wasn't but sixteen."

"Anyway, he went out in a huff when we got tickled and said he was going fishing with Ivan. He ain't here so I guess he's fishing," Midge said.

"Tickled?" Catherine asked.

"He said something like this, 'I do think she knows where the body is and the three O'Shea sisters have made a pact to never tell. I don't know if I could go into a marriage with a woman who didn't share everything with me.' That's when we got tickled and laughed our fool heads off," Midge said.

Catherine's world exploded around her. Marriage? Have to tell it all? Bits and pieces of the past several weeks flew in circles like they'd been picked up by an Arkansas tornado and it was carrying them off to parts unknown before she could collect them into a sensible sentence.

"Anyway, we came to see what is going on," Connie said.

"What else did he tell you?" She asked, cautiously.

Birdy told her what he'd said about Bridget's husband.

"That's the truth," Catherine said.

"Where is he?" Birdie asked.

It wasn't that Catherine wouldn't speak. It was that she couldn't. Not one thing would come from her mouth even though she opened it several times.

"Hey, we wouldn't take that kind of treatment and we don't care where he is. You don't have to answer that. We've barged in here like we knew you and demanded answers to questions we have no right asking," Birdy finally said.

"It's just that Quincy is like a brother to all of us. We've run these beaches since we were just kids, barely out of nappies. When he said in so many words that he really had fallen for you, we just wanted to get to know you better. We've been talking about it all afternoon so we just figured you would be as anxious to get to know us. We didn't think about the way we've rushed in here all friendly. We've intruded badly, haven't we?" Midge said.

"If you want us to leave, we will," Connie said.

"Please don't. Please stay and visit. I've never been alone in my whole life. Momma and Papa were there when I was little. I have a sister a year younger than me. That would be Alice. And one a year younger than her, Bridget, the one with the missing husband and a baby on the way. Bridget divorced him on desertion and took back her own name so that's causing a stink. Alice has always been different and don't give a royal rat's hind end what anyone says. This has been the longest day I've ever spent, so don't go."

She went on to tell them about falling asleep and waking up to a mad old hornet.

"I reckon that he figured out his feelings while you were sleeping," Birdy said.

Connie got up to pour coffee. "And he don't know how to face them."

"And you?" Birdy asked. "It's personal and you don't have to answer it."

"Do you have past secrets you didn't share with your husbands? That's personal and you don't have to answer it, either," Catherine said.

"Of course. The past is the past. From the time you say 'I do' then you don't keep big secrets. Little ones are all right. Ain't no use in worryin' Ivan when I have to knock some sense into one of the boys, but big ones you share and that makes a good marriage. What happened before the 'I do,' now that's a different matter. You think Quincy is going to tell you every minute of his past life? I don't think so, darlin'. Parts he can't tell because it was his job. Parts he won't because it will embarrass him. And other parts he won't because it would hurt his relationship with you." Birdy said.

Well, now, that's a new way of thinking, Catherine thought as she sipped coffee. To start with a clean slate and go forward, forgetting the past. That really would make a good marriage. Lord, she wished her mother was alive so she could ask her if she'd kept things from her father, Patrick. That was the big hold back in falling completely for Quincy. He was intelligent, handsome, kind, considerate, all the things she liked in a man and he made her heart float. She'd love to wake up every morning with him beside her.

Connie broke into Catherine's vision of Quincy asleep on the pillow in the same bed. "So you've eaten two cookies and we've given you time to think."

Catherine blushed.

"Bet you weren't thinking of making gumbo for dinner tomorrow, were you?" Midge teased.

She could love these women, she decided. They were open, honest and friendly.

"No, I wasn't. Actually I was thinking about Quincy's eyelashes when he's asleep," she admitted part of it anyway.

Midge patted her arm. "I knew it."

They talked until midnight and by the time they headed home, Catherine had three new friends of a caliber she didn't know existed outside of blood kin. They were Irish, hot tempered, hard working and passionate just like her and she truly did wish she could move to Florida.

She walked them to the truck. Birdy hugged her like a daughter, something Catherine had missed sorely since her own mother had died.

Just as Birdy got into the vehicle she whispered in her ear. "I don't know if my sister's husband is in hell or heaven so I can say truthfully that I don't know where he is, but I do know he is pushin' up daisies and I'm damn sure not sorry that's where he is," she said.

"And that, darlin', is one of those little secrets I will not share with Ivan," Birdy whispered back.

CHAPTER SIXTEEN

When Catherine awoke the next morning it was to the mixed aromas of frying bacon and coffee drifting from the kitchen into her bedroom. Either Birdy and the girls had come back, which was a very pleasant idea, or else Quincy had come home hungry. She crawled out of bed, got dressed, braided her hair, leaving it in ropes down her back, and followed her nose to the kitchen.

"Good morning," he said.

"Is it?" She asked.

"So are you mad at me?"

"We're back to answering questions with questions?"

"Okay, I deserve it for leaving you alone like that but I had to work some things out and I needed distance away from you to get it done." He piled bacon on a plate and cut a loaf of bread into inch thick slabs to dip in an egg, milk, sugar and cinnamon mixture before frying in the iron skillet.

"That looks good," she said.

"I had mail from my father this morning when I stopped by the store on my way home. I'm being recalled in a week instead of two weeks. You can stay the full time if you want," he said.

"Why?"

"Because you like it here. You can stay or feel free to bring your sisters and use the house anytime you like. I'll give you Ivan's address down here so you can let him know if you are going to come down." He heaped her plate with French toast and bacon, handed her the syrup pitcher and put more toast in the skillet to brown.

"Why are you being called back?"

"There's a job in Galveston, Texas. One of those smuggling things we will be investigating. They're setting me up with a place right now. I'm going in as a writer who's going to be living on the beach while I work on my book. I've been in that area before. It's not as pretty as this but it still has salt water."

If she looked in a mirror she was sure there would be a faint green cast to her face and it wouldn't have a thing to do with his cooking. "Are they sending you a wife?"

He filled his plate and joined her at the table. "That's up to them. I can take one or not. My cover won't need one but it never hurts to appear to be married."

"So did you get it worked out, whatever was worrying you last night?" She asked.

"I did," he said.

"Want to talk about it?"

"No, not right now. I'm hungry. I thought maybe we'd ride our bikes down to Ivan's place today and let you meet the ladies."

"They came to see me last night. Birdy, Midge and Connie."

He spewed coffee all over the front of his shirt, hitting the window hard enough that brown streaks ran down the glass. "They did what?"

She stifled a giggle. "We had a great time. They brought cookies and I made coffee. They stayed until midnight. That Birdy is an outspoken woman and I appreciate a person who says what's on their mind."

Let Quincy chew on that a while rather than running off to figure out what he feels instead of saying it outright. But then what would I do with it if he did come right out and tell me he'd fallen for me?

"So do you want to visit them?" He asked.

"Not especially. I'd rather spend the day with you. Let's explore the cove. We've only been a quarter of a mile down the beach on foot. Is there a boat we can go out in? I've

never been out in a boat. Can that be arranged?"

"It can. Ivan has a small one we could use
to putter around in the cove and maybe go
down to Pensacola Bay," he said.

"I'll pack a picnic. A loaf of bread, chunk
of cheese, what else will we need?"

"Fresh water, some of those oranges I
bought this morning," he said, hoping that
the McCleary ladies hadn't spilled the
beans.

After breakfast they loaded the bicycle
baskets and set off to the south on a road
barely more than a path. Clouds gathered
in the blue sky but they weren't threatening. Palm trees waved in the breeze. A mile
down the path they came to a dock where
several small boats waited. Quincy explained
that the fishermen kept smaller rigs to get
them back and forth if they needed something when they were out in the deep water.
He went to a small craft, no more than
twenty feet long.

"Ivan bought this motor since I was here
last. He told me all about it last night while
we were making a good shrimp haul. It's an
Evinrude knuckle buster. I should have told
you to bring some bandages because Richard said the first six months they had the
thing, he kept busting his knuckles just get-

ting it started," Quincy talked as he worked.

He cranked the wooden handle on top of the motor and jerked his hand back quickly. "Aha, beginner's luck, but I'll tell Richard I'm just faster than he is."

He grabbed the handle and before long they were moving along slowly around the tip of land and into Pensacola Bay. At noon he brought the boat to shore where they both got wet up to their knees pushing it into the sand far enough to secure it to a palm tree. While she spread out the quilt, he carried in the picnic supplies and they had lunch, tossing bits of bread to the birds.

"You've been quiet since breakfast," he said.

"I didn't want to spoil the beauty with words."

"Is that the truth or have we already run out of things to talk about in just three days?"

"What do you want to talk about? We can always redo the five or ten question rule or you can just ask me whatever you want."

"What's your favorite color?"

"That's a real difficult thing to answer," she said.

"Do you just not want to talk to me? Are you mad because I left you alone for the night?"

"No and no. My favorite color as in what? Right now my favorite is the color of that sky up there. It's so peaceful, I'm thinking of choosing wallpaper with a background in that color for the hotel lobby. But if you're asking me that because you are going to purchase a lovely blouse for me, then don't buy that. I'd look like I'd been soaked in bleach in such a pale color. For clothing my favorite color is green. I dearly love red but I would never wear it. Red hair and red clothing do not go together. I'd like red for a sofa for the living room. A nice deep burgundy red that warms the room up by just being there. I also like dark brown like your eyes however I'm thinking you choose grays and blacks because of your hair and that's what I'd choose for you to wear as well but I love the chocolate brown of your eyes. So that wasn't just a throw it out there, get an answer in one word question."

He loved the sound of her voice and thought hard about another question that would keep her talking. "What's your favorite food?"

"Right now it's shrimp or this homemade bread or maybe cheese. Tomorrow it might be chocolate pie. I like good food and I enjoy cooking. I am capable of talking about something other than myself, Quincy."

"Okay then, let's talk politics. Are you aware of just how many soldiers have come home from the war and how many of them are going to be looking for work? Baxter was just one of many who'll be landing in Huttig because there's a saw mill, but there won't be work. I saw the production and the lack of orders that are coming in. Do you know what's going to happen to that little town?"

"From my favorite color to politics and unemployment. That is a jump," she said.

"I realize you are a woman and probably not interested in such things."

"How dare you suggest I'm only interested in wallpaper and giggling. I am totally aware of what's about to happen. Huttig is going to keep being a town because that's where the mill is whether it's big or small. I'm not totally unaware that prices have risen terribly over the past five years. The beds we bought for replacement at the hotel five years ago now cost more than twice as much. Exact on groceries? Seventy–nine percent in the past five years. The last article I read said that the cost of living was up ninety-nine percent and there were four million soldiers looking for work. However, since there's not a need for as much war machinery there is no work for those men.

I'm well aware of our country and the politics. My father was Irish and there was nothing he didn't keep up on concerning this country and he was very vocal. We might be women but we aren't stupid."

"Guess I stepped right up to the plate and asked for that, didn't I?" Quincy asked.

"Begged for it. And while we're on the subject of unemployment and politics, what's going on about this thing everyone is talking about concerning the red scare."

"Where did you hear about that?"

"I read the newspapers. The whole country is up in arms about the Bolsheviks taking over our country and everyone is starting to look at his neighbor like he's a monster. What happens to the little towns when all this blows out of proportion?"

"I imagine everyone will begin to wonder if their neighbor is in some secret Bolshevik organization. Can't you just see Mabel trying to screen everyone who comes into Huttig hunting for a job to see if they're communist? At least there are not radical parades in the little towns like there are in New York City and Boston. I don't know where this is all going to end but I do know the world as we knew it will cease to be and there will be a lot of changes," Quincy said.

"I kind of liked it the way it was. Neighbors being there for you and folks not having to second guess every single thing that happens. Even though Mabel drives me crazy I know who she is and what she'll do," Catherine said.

"None of us like change but we're still in the growing stages in this country. It hasn't been but fifty years since the Civil War. Look how far we've come in that time. Growth is painful sometimes," he said.

"Are we still talking politics or have we moved on to personal things?" She asked.

"Both. What're your predictions for the next twenty years? You are the clairvoyant Irish witch," he smiled.

She could have stopped all discussion right then and kissed him a dozen times. She must never let him know how his smile affected her, or the way it sent her into a tailspin straight for disaster.

"I predict that we will leave this beach and enjoy the rest of this week of bliss then you will go on your job to Galveston and I'll go back to running a hotel. I predict that this red scare will continue for another twenty years and there will be lots of businesses and friendships ruined because of it. The government will have big meetings and all the big wigs will discuss it to death and finally one day it will go away and in fifty years it'll just be a page in the history books. But while it's going on it's going to create havoc."

"That's not predictions. That's just what is probably going to happen," he said. He didn't want to go to the next assignment and leave her in Huttig at the hotel. He wanted her to go with him forever, amen, but how did he approach her with such a ridiculous question? She'd laugh him out of the entire state of Florida.

She threw herself backward on the quilt and shut her eyes tightly. "For that I shall have to consult my inner witch. She says that I'm not a big enough witch to predict twenty years into the future. She says I have to keep it within the next twenty-four hours."

She opened her eyes to see him smiling again. What she was about to do was so far removed from socially acceptable that she feared her mother would rise up out of her grave and haunt her for it. But evidently he wasn't going to speak his mind so she'd have to take the initiative.

Looking right into his eyes and not blinking she said, "I predict that in the next ten minutes you are going to forget that silly notion about being a gentleman and kiss me. I predict that you are going to ask me to marry you and we're going to catch the last train of the day out of Avalon Beach because once you ask me to marry you it wouldn't be right for us to stay together in a house without a chaperone. I predict that we'll go back to Huttig and tell my sisters. You'll stay a night at the Commercial and I'll get my things packed and we'll get married at the El Dorado courthouse when we go through there. Then we'll go to Little Rock and on to Galveston. It can be a working honeymoon and my first detective case. Of course, I could be dead wrong, in which case you'll probably stutter and stammer around trying to tell me I'm all wrong and turn six shades of red."

He leaned in for the kiss. "You're not wrong."

When they broke away, she sat up and grinned at him.

"I fought it tooth, nail and eyeball but I've fallen in love with you, Catherine O'Shea. But before I propose I want to get one thing out of the way for all eternity. I would like you to be honest with me and tell me exactly what you know about Ralph's disappearance for my benefit only. It will never go further than this beach right here. You have my promise."

"Okay, but first, you tell me how many

women there have been in your life. I want to know the exact number of those who you were not a gentleman with and that's just for my benefit so I'll know how much experience I'm getting when I say yes after you propose to me," she said.

He stared at her, long and hard, counting in his mind the number of women she was interested in knowing about. "What has that to do with anything? That's in the past and I give you my word that I'll be faithful. You are the only woman I want, forever, Catherine. I want to go to sleep with you beside me. I want to wake up with you there. I want you to be the mother of my children. I love you."

"I love you, too, Quincy. And darlin' I've fought it harder than you'll ever know. But let's leave the past alone for both of us. You keep whatever secrets you have and I'll do the same. From this day on, there will be no secrets. We'll be honest and discuss everything. I give you my word that I really don't know where Ralph is, heaven or hell or somewhere in between. I just hope he's pushin' up daisies."

He kissed her again. "Will you marry me?"

"Yes, I will." She tangled her hands into his hair and settled closer to him for another kiss.

He kept her in his arms and whispered. "The last train leaves at eight o'clock. We'd better get back if we're going to make it. You sure you want a court house wedding?"

"I've never been more sure of anything in my life. Promise me that we can come back here every so often and remember that it was here I quit fighting against my heart and soul. This is where I finally admitted I'm in love with you and probably have been since the day you got out of the sheriff's car."

He held her tightly. "Darlin' you have my promise on that."

ABOUT THE AUTHOR

Award-winning author **Carolyn Brown** has written over thirty books. She and her husband, Charles, live in Texas and Oklahoma. *Pushin' Up Daisies* is her thirty-second book for AVALON and the first in the *Black Swan Historical Romance* series. *To Believe, The Dove, To Commit, To Trust, Evening Star, Sweet Tilly, Morning Glory, Promises, The PMS Club, Redemption, Chances, Trouble in Paradise, Absolution, Choices, The Wager, Augusta, Garnet, Gypsy, Velvet, Willow, Just Grace, Maggie's Mistake, Violet's Wish, Emma's Folly, Lily's White Lace, The Ivy Tree, All the Way from Texas, The Yard Rose, That Way Again, A Falling Star,* and *Love Is* are also available.